# THE

# LONG JOURNEY

# HOME

Clifton LaBree

Published by
Fading Shadows Imprint
New Boston, New Hampshire, USA


ISBN-10: 1-943329-27-3
ISBN-13: 978-1-943329-27-4


Cover Design by Vivian LaBree

Dedicated to my wife Pauline, and my family, with thanks for all their support and encouragement.

# Chapter One

May 1745

The lumbering French merchant ship sailed into the calm blue waters of the Bay of Fundy under full sails in search of the narrow channel between two prominent pieces of land that give access to the Minas Basin in the heart of Acadia. As far as the eye could see, trees and stumps had been removed from the rich soil to make room for bountiful harvests of potatoes, turnips, flax and squash. The harvest of meadow hay from the low-lying lands for the expanding beef and dairy herds was now in progress.

The ship entered the Basin, turned to the starboard near a place called Grand Pre and dropped anchor next to a small loading dock built out into the water. To the west of the ship, row upon row of apple trees were in full bloom. The productivity of the Acadia apple orchards were praised throughout the new land by those who had experienced them. The white and pink blossoms blanketed the hillside as far as the eye could see. The simple beauty of the agrarian scene touched the hearts of those about to depart the ship. They were impressed by the vast evidence of the labor of those who had preceded them to this land of opportunity. A new life with roots in the dark soil of Acadia was about to begin.

A tall, broad-shouldered man with black hair tied in a tight knot viewed the scene through dark eyes with deep lines around them. He walked with a limp, clinging to the rail of the ship with his wife. She stood straight and proud beside her husband, coming up to his chin. She had a dark complexion

1

with prominent cheek bones and luminous eyes that were always searching her surroundings. Her Delaware Indian heritage was evident in her decorated shirt and pants of soft doeskin. She was beautiful by any standard applied to her and beloved by those who knew her. He placed an arm around her waist and pointed to the log-reinforced sod dikes around the shore of the tidal basin. The reclaimed land from the sea was very productive.

"Our land grant touches the shore of the Minas Basin where we'll be able to do the same thing once we get established," he told her in a strong English voice. "This will be a place where we can live in peace and raise our child that you are now carrying. How proud I am to be your husband."

She looked up into his eyes and smiled. "It is time for you to put to rest those ugly images of battles on the frontier. My brave French soldier deserves to have more peace and harmony in his life, and I will pray for the strength to make that possible," she answered in plain English she had been taught by Moravian missionaries who came to her Delaware village on Lake Ontario near Fort Niagara where he had been stationed.

He returned her smile and kissed her tenderly on the forehead. The deep set to his eyes and the harsh lines around his mouth began to disappear that day he resigned as a soldier in the French Marines under Marquis de Montcalm. He had applied for a grant of land in the maritime province of Nova Scotia. The French portion of Nova Scotia was known as Acadia and was famous for its unlimited codfish catches from the sea and rewarding harvests from the rich red soil.

Abel LeClair had come to the new land as a twenty-year-old marine. His parents had died in France from smallpox. With no family ties to hold him back, he rose to the rank of sergeant after serving two years fighting British forces on the new frontier. The opportunity to cross the Atlantic to New France sounded like an exciting adventure. His military skills were used against the British and in subduing the native peoples who were simply defending their lands against strong western armies. Abel's sense of fairness revolted against such missions.

Sergeant LeClair had been given the mission of escorting a group of Christian Indians from their village on the Ohio River to Fort Niagara on the shore of Lake Ontario. The leader of their group was a Delaware woman with the Christian name of Marie Tanner. Her Delaware name was Iowana, "Whispering Wind." Sergeant LeClair fell in love with her the moment he laid eyes on her.

A year later, he had been seriously wounded in an ambush by Mohawk Indians with a shot through his left leg that shattered his thigh bone, and one in the stomach. The stomach wound healed without complications at Fort Niagara. The wounds on his leg had left it two inches shorter than the other, which made him walk with a pronounced limp. In time he could correct that with properly made shoes. The wound prohibited him from carrying out his duties as an enlisted officer, so he resigned from the service.

The resignation acted as a catalyst for his marriage to Marie, the love of his life, and for his dream of owning a piece of land in the new world. Most of his French friends planned to make their fortune on the frontier and then return to France to live a better life. He had nothing waiting for him back in the old country. The chance to own a piece of land that belonged to him, where he could reap the rewards of his labor were the fulfillment of all his hopes and dreams. With his beautiful wife, two months pregnant, it was an answer to his prayers.

Suddenly, Abel spotted his best friend, John Boisvert, standing at the loading dock, scanning the people on board the ship. John had left the French Army to homestead land in Acadia. He was responsible for obtaining the grant of thirty acres for Abel and enthusiastically told him that it was a good place to settle down and raise a family.

Abel pointed to John on the dock. "Oh, Marie, that's our friend and neighbor. You must remember him. He was my superior officer at Niagara when I was first stationed there. He was the one who helped to settle your group of Christian Indians at a nearby village on Lake Ontario."

"Yes, I remember him as a very kind man," she replied, observing him closely.

As soon as the gangplank was put in place, people began to exit the ship. Abel and Marie carried everything they owned in three leather bags and a large trunk which held, among other things, his prized carbine musket.

John ran to greet them as they stepped ashore. "Welcome to Acadia, Abel and Marie. It's so nice to see familiar faces. When your trunk comes ashore we'll put it in my wagon." He shook hands with Abel and embraced Marie. "I can see that this lovely lady has already worked her magic on you, Abel. The sooner you put those dark memories in the past, the better you'll feel. Acadia has already transformed me. I'm anxious to show you the grant of land you have next to mine on the shore of Minas Basin."

"It's nice to see you again, Lieutenant, or is it John?" Abel replied.

John lifted a hand up to Abel. "Listen, Abel. We left our rank back at Fort Niagara." There was an impish air about the tall, lanky man who inspired excellence in his command. "Of course there may be times when tempers flare and we curse one another, but friendship will override any disagreements."

Marie liked John's nonchalant attitude towards life. He was good for her Abel who had a tendency to be too serious and demanding of himself. "You're correct. It's nice to see a familiar face. My husband has been looking forward to this day for a long time. I didn't expect to see such a beautiful place."

Two sailors carried a large trunk down the plank. John pointed to the wagon where they deposited the trunk in the bed. Marie and Abel carried their three bags to the wagon and climbed into the seat beside John. He had folded a heavy flax blanket and placed it on the plank to ease the bumps on his new passengers. The black Belgian draft horse set a slow pace down a well-worn cart track along the shore of Minas Basin. John pointed out several log cabins in different stages of completion. Some had grass roofs.

"When you're ready to cut the logs for your cabin," John told him, "several of our neighbors will join in to erect it. You can borrow my Belgian to drag the logs from the forest to your building site. I have all the tools you'll need to cut the trees into suitable lengths. At the same time, you'll want to prepare a large amount of firewood for this coming heating season. I will have a cord or so to start you out for the winter."

"How are the winters here, John?" Abel asked.

"Naturally, they're cold like Fort Niagara, but not as much snow. Within our farming community of French settlers at Acadia, there are those who will sell or bargain with you for tools, animals, seed for crops, and hay. The first two seasons are the hardest, but we can at least labor in an atmosphere of peace," John said to encourage the two newcomers.

An hour later, John was excited to point out the thirty acre land tract assigned to Abel. It contained about six hundred feet of frontage on the north shore of Minas Basin which had a very high tide of almost forty feet. There was a chance for Abel to expand the acreage in the low-lying marsh lands by building dikes out of logs and sod. The parcel was rectangular in shape. Some of the land bordering the shore front had already been cleared except for stumps. The higher elevations were covered with spruce, balsam fir, and some white pine trees of various sizes suitable for lumber and firewood. There was a hill to the north of the Bay which Abel spotted as an ideal location for apples.

A tent had already been erected by John for the newcomers to use while their cabin was being constructed.

Abel was quick to note that the sun would rise directly over the Basin, spreading warmth over the area first thing in the morning. He made the decision to orient the front of the cabin to capture the first rays of sunshine. It was a simple decision made on a whim, but it was the first for their own piece of land. It was an empowering moment he frequently recalled as the years rolled by.

That first year was filled with back-breaking labor from sunup to sundown, building their two-room log cabin with the southern end erected at a tunnel he had excavated into the hillside for a root cellar and the storage of smoked meat and fish. In those latitudes a family had to be diligent in preparing for the long winters that were a natural part of their lives.

While Abel concentrated on the construction of the cabin and root cellar, John and his fourteen-year-old-son, Jodi, prepared several acres of the open land and planted potatoes, squash, and turnips. Several neighboring fishermen volunteered to supply them with a winter's supply of dried cod and salmon for storage in their cellar.

The community spirit impressed Abel and Marie. Most of their neighbors were French and Catholic, with a few Protestant communicants. Traditionally the two factions did not get along, but, here in Acadia, there was a spirit of brotherhood that transcended the differences. Their status as immigrants that had crossed the Atlantic to establish a new way of life in this land of plenty united them. Just surviving was an accomplishment. To prosper usually requires the helping hands of friends and neighbors. Collectively more could be done than was possible with the sum of individuals doing the same tasks.

Abel and his pregnant wife moved into their new cabin the end of July. They celebrated their occupancy with a toast of well-aged apple cider. Sitting across from each other at the fresh hewn table next to the fireplace, Abel was the first to speak.

"John told me that this was a potent drink with a kick, so we'll go easy on it," he smiled, pouring a small amount into each of their tin cups. "A toast to my lovely wife who has made my life worthwhile."

"To my husband who has labored so hard. Our new home is a symbol of the roots we will plant here in this peaceful place called Acadia." She took a small sip of the liquid and shuddered, "Oh, it's strong like vinegar."

He laughed, swallowing a mouthful. "It takes a strong constitution to handle this stuff. I didn't expect to complete the cabin and the hillside root cellar this soon. The crops John and Jodi planted are looking healthy and vigorous. I'm anxious to take some time checking the Basin for fish. I remember two years ago when I crossed the Atlantic we jigged for codfish, catching a large amount of them in a short time. The water was filled solid with cod. We appreciate the offer of our fishermen friends, but I want to make certain that we will have enough food for the long winter months ahead."

"While you were in the forest beyond the hill, I had a visit from John's wife, Rosalee. She said she was weaving some blankets and flax cloth for our use. It was one of the things we did not have room to bring with us. The skins from two deer you had shot are almost ready to make winter footwear. I've finished smoking the venison. It is now in the cool root cellar. I really like the cellar being at the rear of the house. It's cool, and the food will last a long time."

"Our decision to homestead here in Acadia has been a good choice. Thank God for friends like John Boisvert. He was an excellent Army officer with a reputation of carrying out orders efficiently. The men liked him for his concern of their welfare. I'm surprised the Army let him retire," he mused. "It was easy for me with this bum leg, but I don't complain."

She mirrored his mood and said, "Rosalee informed me that the British control portions of this land and that there was some concern about the future. What do you think, Abel?"

"The French and the British are competing for control of a continent. At times the struggle has been vicious. I'm hopeful that both nations will settle their differences in peace so that they can live side by side. The Scotch-Irish have been here as long as the French. The tug of war that has been taking place for years between them without reaching a suitable conclusion should prove that force of arms does not advance the position of either country. After all, we should be able to govern ourselves as free people separate from the mother countries in Europe. I've known several English soldiers that had the same feelings. I have no animosity towards them."

Marie listened to her husband knowing that he valued his freedom to live in peace more than life itself. She remained silent, praying that the two nations had similar views. She privately feared that peace might become illusive and temporary. She had personally experienced periods of violence interrupted by short durations of peaceful coexistence. It was a cycle that followed her native Delaware tribe as well as the white men who had come to the new land. She had hoped and dreamed like her husband, but experience warned her to be prepared for the unexpected, and she was angry that she entertained such thoughts.

She was reassured with their reception by the community of farmers. Normally mixed marriages would be unacceptable, or at the least, tolerated with "stiff correctness". If this chapter of their lives proved to be an unhappy one, her beloved husband was prepared to take her back to France, a move she strongly dismissed. She was determined to make this beautiful place by the sea not just a place to reside, but a home where body and soul could find peace, contentment, and a sense of achievement for the hard work both individuals had committed to its success.

Slowly the warm days of summer gave way to shorter days with a distinct drop in temperature. Winter was waiting for its introduction. Deep snow, fierce winds, and plunging temperatures were the norm in those northern latitudes. Wise inhabitants spent most of their time preparing for winter, struggling to endure winter, and recovering from the trauma of winter. The harshness of the region's weather tempered the character of the hardy Acadians. Fighting the elements could be an indication of unpreparedness and a frightening experience. Most simply accepted the hardship as a way of life. To treat it differently was to fail and failure had no future.

As Marie's time to give birth approached, Abel questioned his ability to assist his wife in delivering the baby. To his relief, Rosalee had insisted that Jodi stay with the LeClairs when her time was near. When Marie began her birthing pains, Jodi could run to get his mother.

That moment came in the middle of the night during a raging snow storm early in January 1746. Jodi and Abel were woken by a piercing scream from Marie's lips. Jodi was sleeping fully clothed in front of the fireplace on a bear rug. Startled by the announcement, he threw on his coat and darted out the door to fetch his mother.

Abel first went to Marie's side. She was covered with sweat. "The time is close, Abel. I felt the contractions all evening. Do not be afraid; we are about to bring a new life into our small world."

He clung to her sweating hand. "Jodi has already gone for Rosalee. I'm going to get the fire going better and put on some water to heat." She was in a room off the great room in the cabin. Some light shown from the fireplace, but more was needed. He lit several candles around the room including two beside Marie's bed before rushing to place more dry logs on the glowing embers of the fire. It was cold outside. Abel was thankful for the warmth and comfort of their cabin nestled into the hillside.

Marie had already laid out baby clothes and blankets on the chair beside the bed. She had also collected a large supply of soft dry sphagnum moss from the forest in the summertime for use as diapers for the baby. Bending over his wife, Abel counted the seconds between the painful contractions. When Rosalee arrived, he breathed a sigh of relief, telling her that the contractions were about three minutes apart.

Rosalee gently escorted Abel out of the room, telling him to brew some tea and to sit down to drink some. Marie was very much alert and in control of her baby. Traditionally, Delaware women gave birth in the fields or in the forest by themselves with a very short interruption of normal activity.

In his heart, Abel was hoping for a son, but he was willing to concede that a daughter like his beloved Marie would brighten their world. Little girls have won their fathers' hearts since the beginning of time. He drank his second cup of hot tea when Rosalee entered the room and stood beside the fireplace. She then turned to him and said, "Abel, you have a strong baby boy," passing the child wrapped in several layers of blankets to him. "Your wife was very strong. She's resting easy now."

The first thing Abel noticed about his son was his tiny fingers that clasped his thumb. He softly cried out, "Thank you, God."

# Chapter Two

The new addition to the LeClair household was christened Drew Abel LeClair. That winter, the snow was very deep and the temperature hovered below zero degrees for days at a time. Shortly after the birth of the baby, Abel constructed a small cradle out of white ash he had placed in the root cellar earlier in the summer to dry. The cradle rocked little Drew to sleep every evening in front of the fireplace, the center of their lives during the long winter months.

Within their small rural community of farmers, there was very little contact with settlers from Scotland and Ireland who made up the majority of the population. The French had been in Acadia for over a century. The struggle for control of the continent continued unabated with intermittent warfare between the two factions. France controlled sections of the Maine coast as well as large portions of New Brunswick and Cape Breton Island. The English were increasingly distrustful of the Roman Catholic French in their midst. Most of the LeClair's neighbors were Catholic. Abel and Marie were Protestants.

The uncertainty of the political situation was of great concern, but it did not alter their desire to put down firm roots for the future. They loved their plot of land, and their neighbors accepted their sincere effort to be a part of the community, regardless of religious differences.

Almost a year had passed since the massive Fort Louisbourg at the southern tip of Cape Breton Island capitulated to the British after a lengthy siege. The capture of the stronghold by militia from New England was a surprise to the whole world. The fort guarded the entrance to the Saint Lawrence River valley and ultimately controlled access to all of eastern and northern Canada. Militias from Massachusetts Bay Colony and New Hampshire joined forces to strike a blow against the fort. French privateers had been reigning havoc with shipping on the eastern seaboard. Whenever they were confronted with force, they retreated to the protective custody of Fort Louisbourg. Now there was an even stronger English presence in the maritime region of Canada!

Supplies from the Caribbean arrived on a weekly basis at the Basin. Abel stocked up on gunpowder and lead for his pistols and musket carbine. He also traded codfish for glass windows, textile products, and fresh fruit such as bananas and oranges. Rum and molasses were also popular commodities of trade. There was very little manufacturing taking place in Acadia, so metal pots and pans and tea had to be purchased from Europe.

Abel had built a small dock on the shore of the Basin where he could keep his rowboat. Every day during the summer, he fished for cod and haddock which he dried in the open fields before storing them in his cellar for winter consumption and trading for goods the merchant freighters offered.

Aside from the normal summertime activity of fishing, planting, and weeding the crops, Abel was always clearing portions of his land to expand his field crop and apple orchard production. He cleared the trees from the land by attaching a chain or sturdy rope as high up on the tree's bole as possible; then he tipped the tree, roots and all, from the soil. The sturdy Belgian draft horse handled the task with ease. By doing it in the summertime, the soil could be preserved and kicked back into the hole made by the roots. The trees, regardless of species, were cut up into firewood lengths and split to dry properly.

Each year Marie collected seeds from apples they had eaten so that she could plant them in small pans to germinate. Once the plants were a foot or so, they planted them in straight rows up and down the hillside. The prevailing westerly winds helped the bees germinate the apple crop at blossoming time. The layout of the orchard was primarily Marie's project. The orchards in Acadia were the crown jewels of the community of farmers. Apples and apple pies became a staple food for the hardy settlers.

The presence of their son, Drew, made all of their work worthwhile. As the years slowly rolled by, Abel and Marie diligently expanded and improved their productive capacity on their little piece of land. Abel worked from sunup to sundown either in the fields or on the water fishing. When Drew was five years old he was always at his father's side in the fields or on the water in the boat gigging for codfish, enjoying the company of his father.

At this pivotal time in Drew's life, his parents decided that it was important for him to read and write and to study those subjects in which they could obtain adequate teaching materials. There were no organized schools in Acadia at that time. Marie offered to teach Drew, Jodi, and Prudence on a daily basis how to read and write French as well as English. She remembered how the Moravian missionaries had instructed students in her native New York, so she approached the parish priest in Grand Pre for assistance.

Marie was shocked about the reluctance of the priest to help her in any way. Marie and Abel were not Catholics and did not attend Mass. She had expected him to be as forthcoming as the Moravian ministers. She left the priest depressed and, for the first time since they came to Acadia, was uncertain if she and Abel had made a wise decision. There was no warmth or encouragement from the elderly priest. He looked down on her, making her feel unworthy.

Undeterred by the Catholic priest, Marie collected books, paper, ink and other teaching materials from several of the traders who stopped at the dock every week. French and English lessons began that summer and continued every day except Sunday first thing in the morning for Prudence and Drew. Rosalee, who could not write or read either language, accompanied Prudence to the LeClair cabin.

Tensions between the French community in Acadia and the larger population of Scotch-Irish settlers in Nova Scotia was increasing every day. For decades France and England had vied for control of North America. Each laid claim to the same land with valid credentials to back up their claim. Time and again the conflict that boiled in Europe continued in North America until a temporary truce was signed by dignitaries in Europe. The conflict eased in the area of New France and along the eastern seaboard, but it never completely stopped. The contest was fueled partly by the desire of British subjects to settle on their grants of land with the expectations that they were the supreme owners and masters of their domain. Ownership was a treasured concept that was not reciprocated by the Native Americans who could never comprehend the idea that the land, like the sun and water and the air they breathed, could be owned. They visualized it as a birthright.

The land controversy fueled the atrocities committed by both sides, and it collided with the French philosophy of making fortunes on furs, timber, and codfish so that they could return to their original homes in France. Consequently the French assimilated more successfully with the Indians than the British.

When Marie and Abel journeyed to Acadia to begin a new life for themselves, they were fully aware of the inherent goals of all parties involved, the French, the British and the Indians. Life on the active frontiers such as Lake Champlain and northern New England was filled with uncertainty. Depraved acts of cruelty were being perpetrated by the French-led Abenaki Indians throughout the region on a daily basis. It was not the kind of place they wanted to homestead. A chance to put down roots in the maritime region seemed a better alternative. There was less conflict and competition for the basic commodity of land.

Their concerns for the area were based on the fact that John and Rosalee had settled in the Acadian farming community. The French claim to Acadia was sound, yet both Abel and John knew that if it came to a contest of arms, the French would lose. France had the best army in the world, but it was woefully inadequate in numbers. Conflicts in Europe prevented them from sending more troops to the new world, so they relied on the native Indians who had successfully terrorized the frontier regions for years. However, the British were capable of sending more troops to the region than the French. That simple fact had always bothered Abel, though he never spoke to Marie about it.

Superior numbers in any contest resulted in victory. The stronger always prevailed...

Abel had disapproved of the vicious type of conflict the French encouraged with the Abenaki. Raids on hapless settlers continued across the broad frontier landscape. Abel came to hate the Jesuit priests who incited the Indians to greater and greater barbarity against the hated English. Abel did not blame the British for hating the French and their associates for their depraved crimes against humanity.

Because Abel was a Protestant, he felt the sting of prejudice in some circles of the French Army. Though it never broke out into the open, there were always whispered words that made him feel less appreciated and second-rate. It was a fact of life in the army – Protestants were never a true part of that brotherhood which existed in all armies of the world. For that he was glad to leave the army.

Before Abel and Marie moved to Acadia there was much soul-searching on Abel's part. To him the most precious thing in the world was the soft-spoken Delaware maiden he had wed. He would do anything to keep her from harm. His best friend, John Boisvert, understood Abel's priorities and was instrumental in their decision to settle in Acadia. John was anxious to share with his friend the peace he knew prevailed in the beautiful Annapolis Valley of Acadia.

Acadia was relatively free of the more intense struggles on the frontiers of Northern New England and the Ohio River Valley. Acadia was remote enough that there was a good chance the conflict would pass by. It was a dream they all prayed for.

When Marie set up her tutoring period in her kitchen, she found that she enjoyed the challenge as much as the two full-time pupils enjoyed the change in their daily routines. By the time fall harvest rolled around, her class had been increased to eight students. She started each student with the alphabet and how to write their names. When she had done that with Prudence, she reduced the name to one syllable for ease of learning. Prudence instantly became Pru to everyone. Abel occasionally related to the students about his experience in France.

14

Winter came quickly to Acadia. Crops were stored in the root cellars and large amounts of dried codfish were placed in storage. There was something satisfying about being prepared for the long winter months. Abel continued to fish even after the first frost.

One day, Abel was out in the Basin close to his dock fishing when a large four-mast ship with several open gun ports entered the Basin and made a complete turn close to the shore all the way around the inland waters. He failed to see any flag or any person on the deck. Ships were not new to the area. He waved several times at the large vessel and never received one in return. A strange feeling came over him.

He said nothing about the incident to Marie, but it bothered him for several days. Later, he spoke to John about the ship. John had replied in a sober voice, "It's probably a privateer, Abel, out searching for opportunities to plunder..." Both soldiers recognized their vulnerability to an armed invasion from any source...

# Chapter Three

Tensions in Acadia were high. The conflict called the Seven Years War in Europe was in full bloom in frontier America. Raids by the French and their allies, the Abenaki and Penobscot Indians, were dispensing terror along the northern New England frontier with little organized resistance by the British.

The Ohio Valley was claimed by the French, and they began building forts at the mouth of the Niagara River on Lake Ontario, Fort Frontenac on Lake Erie, as well as several forts and stockades down the Ohio. France was prepared to defend its claim against all trespassers. The victor would end up retaining control of all the lands already settled and those unexplored acres to the west. The mood of the settlers in Acadia was one of anxious anticipation.

John and Abel had kept in touch with events on a daily basis. Trading ships visited Minas Basin frequently. Abel collected newspapers and questioned the sailors for news and gossip. News conveyed by mouth was always subject to confirmation. His favorite source of information was a newspaper called *COASTAL BEACON* from Portsmouth, New Hampshire, published by Daniel Cullen. The publisher was a loyal colonist with independent views based on facts, not hearsay. Marie knew Daniel Cullen's wife from shared experiences in the northern frontier.

Ever since the British captured Fort Louisbourg, their influence in Acadia had increased considerably. The fort had been an active center for French privateers who had raided along the coast. The latest news from the colonies involved an international incident when a young Virginia militia officer,

Major George Washington, attacked and killed a French patrol in western Pennsylvania. The inexperienced militia officer set the stage for a much enlarged and more intense struggle for a continent. Abel read a short description of what took place in the *Beacon* and quickly hitched the Belgian to the wagon and left to speak to John. Drew went along with him, noting that his father was preoccupied and quieter than usual.

Normally they talked freely about crops, fishing, and comments about the large number of trading ships that visited Acadia. Father and son enjoyed each other's company. Drew had grown into a sturdy eight-year-old with broad shoulders and an easy walk like his father. Drew looked like his mother with slightly lighter skin color. His prominent cheek bones gave him a more mature look than his years. His father was proud of his son and frequently told him so.

"Is something wrong, Father? Ever since you received that information packet from the supply ship, you've been quieter than usual. Even Mother is concerned," Drew told him.

Abel clasped his arm, giving him an affectionate squeeze. "I'm sorry if I've given you and your mother cause to worry," he responded in English. "I can tell you that I read something that I want to discuss with John. He was my superior officer and has his own source of information that may be more up-to-date. I wanted to hear what he has to say about events taking place between the French and English. I haven't wanted you or your mother to worry. We settled here in Acadia because the French have been here and in many parts of Canada for a long time. I believe we're safe on our own piece of land. This farm is something I've always dreamed of having. My folks died before I left France as a soldier in the marines, so I had no intention of returning to France. Even if I did, there is very little land available for people like me."

"Why don't some people like Mother or me the same way they like you, Father?" Drew asked.

His father was quick to reply, "As you get a little older, son, you're going to realize that most people will like you or your mother because you're kind and caring people. We should be judged by what's in our hearts, not by the color of our skin. You have the blood of my French family and your mother's

Delaware ancestry which includes wise chiefs and leaders of tribal councils. There will always be those who will look upon you as inferior, and I beg of you to ignore their opinions and have nothing to do with them. Be your true self and listen to that little voice inside of you. That little voice will never lead you astray. Hold your head high, son."

"Mother tells me things like that, too," Drew added, watching a merchant sloop glide past them on the Basin. "My best friends are Prudence and Jodi. He's sweet on a girl in the Perreault family."

Abel smiled. "There comes a time in every man's life when young ladies become more interesting. It'll happen to you, Drew."

Drew listened to his father and mused about the time when he and Pru went up to the top of the hill behind the cabin to pick blueberries together. The conversation had been a little troubling to him. Pru had told him that her mother was frightened at what the British might do if they overpowered the French in Canada. "She cries often in the middle of the night. My father tries to reassure her that they will be safe regardless of what takes place. He often says that the Acadians are simple farmers, not participants in the war."

Drew had asked her, "Are you frightened, Pru?"

"Oh yes, even though I don't understand what's going on," she replied. "You and your father may be treated differently because you are not Catholics."

"Father believes that our religious beliefs should be our private right. My mother agrees with him. Father never talks about things that would give us worry, and wants to protect us from anything that might make us unhappy. Your father wants the same things for your family, too, Pru."

She sat on a rock and stared at Drew, kneeling to pick blueberries. "Do you want that for me, too, Drew?"

"Sure, you're my best friend. If you were unhappy, I'd be unhappy, too," he replied, avoiding her stare.

"Did you ever want to kiss me?" she boldly asked.

The question sent off alarm bells inside him. Did she know that he had often wondered about kissing her like his father kisses his mother? He had never dared to tell anyone. How did she know? He stuttered a reply that took all of his courage. "If you want the truth, I used to think that it was a foolish thing only grownups do."

"You're not answering my question, Drew."

He turned away from her because he knew that he was blushing and she would know... "Yes, I've thought about it, have you?"

"Would you like to kiss now?" she asked calmly.

"You mean on your lips..."

"Well of course, Drew. If you want to, I'd let you. We're too young to know what the future is going to be. I can tell you that if you went away I'd miss you a lot and would probably cry for a long time," she exclaimed hesitantly.

Without saying a word, Drew stood up and placed his lips on hers for a second. He did not know what to expect, but he had anticipated more of a reaction than he felt. All he could remember about the act was that her lips had tasted like blueberries they both had been eating.

"What do you think? Tell me the truth, Drew."

"I can't understand what the big fuss is all about," he answered directly. "Your lips are softer than mine, but they still tasted blueberries."

It was not the answer she had expected, but she was satisfied that it was his truthful reaction to the act. She jumped down from the rock to continue picking blueberries, thinking about his response. Suddenly she stood up and said, "I heard my mother and father talking when they didn't think I was listening that when we get older, we might get married. What would you say to that, Drew LeClair?"

She looked him square in the eyes with a determined tilt to her chin. She had been thinking a lot about the questions she asked her eight-year-old friend. Lately she had been experiencing the same anxieties about the future as her parents. She did not understand why, but she perceived in her innocence of ten years of age that if something bothered her parents as consistently as events proved, then it had to be serious.

Pru and Drew had been neighbors and friends ever since birth. They talked a lot together about their language lessons and what their parents discussed. Drew always looked upon Pru as an extended family member. He was kind and unselfish with her and in his innocent ways sort of felt responsible for her. At one time when she was very sick with smallpox he visited her home every day to see how she was doing. At one point he looked at her pale, almost white face and thought she had died. That possibility frightened him.

When she recovered from the illness he picked a large bouquet of wild purple violets. She smiled when he put them in a tin cup of water beside her bed. Her smile pleased him. She was his best friend, and friends take care of each other. Pru was several weeks recovering from the disease. It left several pockmarks on her cheeks which she was self-conscious about. Drew told her that he liked her because she was his best friend and that he would not like her less because the disease left some marks on her face. Her survival from the disease was truly a miracle; most succumbed to the high temperatures. Her mother said that it was a miracle from God, and meant that God had some special reason for her in the future. To Drew, a serious young boy, that status made his friend Pru very special.

Drew was perceptive enough to know that a wrong answer to her question of marriage sometime in the future could hurt her. He didn't want to make her feel bad. "Your question is a serious one that can only be answered when we're older, Pru. My father said people and situations change as they grow older. Things that are important now may not be that way in five to ten years from now..."

"Are you saying yes or no?" She sensed his uncertainty.

"Pru, it cannot be answered because no one knows what the future is. I'll always want to call you my friend. When you're sad, I feel sad, too. When you're happy I'm happy, too. I think that's what being a friend means."

She grinned at how serious he was. "I understand your answer. Are you angry at me for being so personal?"

He looked up at her, for she was an inch taller. "I'm not upset with you, Pru. I listen and think about things our fathers talk about. Things are happening far away that could be harmful to our farms and homes. Both of our parents are concerned about things. Whatever happens, I'll always be your friend, Pru."

She reached out and touched his arm, "Thank you for telling me that, Drew. You're a very kind friend, and I'll never forget..."

One day Marie returned papers the children used for a spelling test. Prudence had been a student for several months and was able to recite and write the alphabet. She had misspelled two words on her paper and was discouraged by the mistakes, hiding her paper in her pocket. Drew offered to walk home with her. His father was helping John pick the last of his apples for the season.

"Why did you almost cry, Pru?" Drew asked casually.

"I didn't almost cry. I was just disappointed with myself, that's all," she exclaimed, embarrassed that Drew had witnessed her displeasure.

Drew thought about these incidents often and wondered what it would be like not to have a friend like Pru. She could run faster than him, and she was able to remember and recite lessons long before he could do the same thing. Sometimes she made him feel ten feet tall, and then other moments she could make him angry. He wondered if that was what his mother and father had gone through.

Abel saw a faraway look in his son's eyes. He had seen that same look on his wife. "You and Pru are doing very well with your school work. Your mother has done a good job with you. It was nice to see Rosalee grow in confidence as she became able to read and write. What a wonderful thing to give the gift of knowledge. Knowledge of any type gives us a wider view of this world we live in."

Drew had heard similar words from his mother. He gazed out into the Basin as they turned into the cart tracks leading to John's cabin. Rosalee and Pru were combing flax fibers, getting it ready to be woven into cloth. Drew joined them while his father walked into the barn to talk with John.

"Hi, John," Abel hailed, grabbing a shovel to help clean out a stall. "I wanted to get your thoughts on what's happening out there."

They finished cleaning the barn and took a seat on a stool next to a feed bin. Abel spoke first. "The butchery taking place on the northern frontiers does not serve the cause of France in the New World. Even Maine has had to build two forts, Halifax and Western, on the Kennebec for protection. We still control Fort Louisbourg on Cape Breton Island. What do you think, John? How do the activities on the Ohio affect us in our little world here in Acadia? I'm getting more and more uneasy about my decision to move here."

"I can't guarantee the future, Abel. For now, I think we'll be okay. The British are building up to push the French out of the Ohio Valley. General Braddock is a good general. He'll lead the charge against the Ohio and will be a formidable enemy for our friends on garrison duty there. Ultimately the Ohio holds the key to France's ability to overcome the power of the Crown. If the British prevail on the Ohio, then they'll eventually roll up the Hudson River-Lake Champlain corridor to Montreal and on to Quebec. Once that is done, they can lay siege to Nova Scotia and Cape Breton, demanding surrender on their own terms…"

Abel agreed with his friend's analysis. "Do you think the British will bother us in Acadia? After all, we've been here for several decades."

"You're asking the impossible, Abel. My gut feeling is they'll allow the French to remain in Acadia as well as the large population in Canada. We've both seen things we disagree strongly with. The French have constantly agitated the Abenaki against the British authority with unspeakable brutality to innocent settlers on the frontier. We've also experienced widespread corruption within the French Army and in the civilian authorities. Corruption is deeply imbedded and is one of the reasons that both of us were glad to resign our commissions. I knew first-hand that many of the British authorities recognize and appreciate the values we Acadians represent. The French have labored long and hard to turn the population hostile against the Crown. As for me, I find no fault with our current status quo. Does this frighten you, Abel?"

Abel stood up to empty his pipe, "I've no fear for myself. If I thought that my family was threatened, I'd abandon my farm and seek refuge back in France or any place that would give us sanctuary. Damn... it would be hard to walk away from the land..., but I'd do it, John."

"I understand, my good friend. I've had similar thoughts myself."

"The French have consistently told us that if we remain supportive, they will protect us. I want to believe that, but I'm skeptical." John was reluctant to mention religion. Since it was at the heart of his anxiety, he shared his frustrations with his best friend. "I speak as a Protestant, John. I want you to know that I value your friendship more than anything else in the world. I lay most of the blame for all the fear and uncertainty squarely on the shoulders of the Catholic clergy. Some are more rabid and bloodthirsty than the natives they urge to greater feats of butchery. If the clergy represent France, then they have lost my support."

"Let's pray for reconciliation. If that happens, our worries are all in vain."

Abel and Drew returned home filled with hope, but the reality of the situation Acadians found themselves gave ample evidence to believe that at some time in the future, either France or England was going to be the supreme ruler of the New World. The days of joint authority were numbered, and Acadia may be changed forever!

# Chapter Four

Those farmers who kept track of events taking place on the western frontier learned that after the winter of 1754-1755, the British sent a large force across the Atlantic under the command of General Braddock. His first duty was to roll back the French improvements on the Ohio River. To everyone's surprise, the French decisively defeated the British regiment, killing Braddock. The victory secured their claim on the territory.

Braddock had laid out a strategy for defeating the French in the New World: attacks on the Hudson Valley-Lake Champlain corridor and securing Acadia and as much of the maritime region as manpower permitted in order to isolate Fort Louisbourg. That summer was a bad year for the British with two exceptions: first, they had successfully stopped the French drive south into the Hudson Valley by winning the Battle of Lake George; and second, they successfully attacked and occupied Fort Beausejours which had ominous repercussions for the Acadians.

Fort Beausejours protected the Nova Scotia frontier of Acadia on the isthmus to New Brunswick. It was located on a hill north of Chignecto Bay. The fort had twenty-four cannons and several mortars manned by several companies of French soldiers and one thousand civilian Acadians. Colonel Robert Moncton sailed from Boston with a force of twenty-three hundred men on May 26, 1755.

The Acadians knew the attack was imminent. The French Army was seriously hampered by ravenous unscrupulous authorities in Canada who robbed the government so much that added forces could not be sent to protect the Acadian farmer, so the Acadians remained in fear of their lives. Their future was squandered by both the French and the British as events would prove. Moncton sailed into Chignecto Bay and captured the fort with a minimum of casualties. The Acadian workers at the fort were sent home with the warning that the British were now in control of Acadia.

Shortly after the capture of the fort, Moncton issued a proclamation to all of the inhabitants of Acadia announcing that they would have to shift their allegiance from France to the British Crown, and that every adult male in the immediate vicinity was ordered to appear at Grand Pre September 2, 1755.

On the appointed day in September, Lieutenant Colonel Winslow, a British regular, appeared at Grand Pre while other units held similar gatherings throughout the region. Winslow began his speech through a French interpreter:

> "French inhabitants of Nova Scotia,
>
> His Excellency the Governor has instructed that we submit to the inhabitants of Acadia the same information such as His Majesty the King has communicated to Him. You should be fully aware of His Majesty's intentions.
>
> We therefore order and strictly enjoin that both old and young men and all lads of ten years to congregate and meet at Grand Pre church on Friday the fifth of September at three o'clock afternoon. There will be no excuse on pain of forfeiting goods and chattels. Thank You."

On the appointed day, Abel, Drew, John and Jodi rode into Grand Pre in Abel's wagon. Almost five hundred men made up the congregation. Colonel Wilson was in his best laced red uniform with several sturdy subalterns gathered around him. He ordered a table to be set up in the middle of the church. Taking his place behind the table, he nodded to his French interpreter and began:

"Gentlemen,--I have received from His Excellency, Governor Lawrence, the King's instructions, which I have in my hand. By his orders you are called together to hear His Majesty's final solution concerning the French inhabitants of Nova Scotia, who for almost a half century have had more indulgence granted them than any of his subjects in any part of his dominions. What use you have made of it you yourselves know best.

The duty I am now upon, though necessary, is very disagreeable to my natural make and temper, as I know it must be grievous to you… But it is…on the orders I shall deliver to you His Majesty's instructions and commands, which are that your lands and tenements and cattle and live-stock of all kinds are forfeited to the Crown… except money and household goods, and that you yourselves are to be removed from this His province……"

The Colonel went on to declare that every effort would be made to keep families together on the same ships; and that they would be protected from molestation while this deportation was taking place. He emphasized that every family could take with them all they were capable of carrying on board the ship. He also wished that wherever they end up they'll be happy and peaceful subjects. Few ever heard the words at the end of the speech. There was a great howl of agony and distress from the assembly of men. The British were determined to bring the population into compliance. All they had to do was sign the oath of allegiance to the British Crown.

When Colonel Winslow finished reading the announcement he stepped around the table asking if anyone had any questions.

Abel stepped forward. "Colonel Winslow, I speak for myself, my family, and my son Drew here with me. I was a sergeant in the French Marines. I resigned after being wounded in the leg. I understand that you have orders that must be obeyed. I've witnessed the treatment of the Acadians by French officials and have been disappointed and most critical of their performance. Since I've been in Acadia, the British officials have been truthful and fair. However, I'm a French subject. I cannot take the oath of allegiance to the Crown because my allegiance is to France, my native land, not to the officials in Canada. Therefore, I refuse to take the oath you offer."

Colonel Winslow looked up at Abel with the broad shoulders, noting the look of determination. "Since you were once a soldier, you must know what orders mean. I do not have any animosity against these hard-working people, and I do not have the authority to change what has been presented to you. If you take the vow of allegiance in writing you may stay and continue working your farm. If not, you and your family will be deported. You may take whatever you can carry, but you forfeit your land, crops, and home. We are not monsters. You have much to lose, Sir. Consider the consequences."

Abel looked defiantly at the British officer. "What price are you willing to pay to take my land? We are not sheep easily led to slaughter. Instead of a bloodbath with losses on both sides, I propose a dual between you and me, winner take all. If I win, the family remains in peace on the land. Remember, I have one bad leg."

The challenge caught Colonel Winslow off guard. He turned pale white and began to stutter. "I cannot accept your duel. I caution you not to revert to violence. I understand your position, but I will follow my orders. Please excuse me."

Abel placed an arm around Drew and turned away from the crowd. John and Jodi quietly walked by his side to the wagon. "I was afraid you were going to do something foolish in there, Abel."

"I had some things in mind," Abel replied. "What are you going to do, John?"

"I don't know," John admitted, still stung by the severity of the new English rulers. "If I have to leave the farm, I'll try again in Maine somewhere near Penobscot Bay. I know several men who have served there in the Army. They all claimed it to be the most peaceful place on the frontier. Right now I'm just too angry to make any rational decisions. One thing is for sure. I'm not going to stockpile any more stuff in my root cellar."

"I've been thinking the same thing," Abel said, climbing into the wagon.

Young Drew had heard the proclamation and knew what it meant to his family and friends who were being forced out of their homes for no just reason. It wasn't fair. "Can't we fight for our rights? You have your musket and two pistols in the trunk, Father."

"If I did not have you and your mother to think about, I'd resist with force," Abel answered with a determined edge to his voice. "I'd lose and probably get killed. The British would bring in more troops, and gun ships could anchor off the coast and bombard our homes and crops at will. No, we could not win even if we are in the right. The strong always win. It's that simple."

The day after the meeting with Colonel Winslow, ships began to congregate in the Basin and Chignecto Bay, waiting for deportees to be brought aboard. Throughout Acadia there was a tremendous cry for justice and for the British to rethink the brutality of their decree. Entire families wept until there were no tears left to shed. No one listened to their pathetic pleas for justice. The whole world was turned upside down. Their peaceful agrarian way of life was terminated by one proclamation written and executed by strangers who had no interest in solving problems other than forcing the Acadians to abandon their land. From that day forward, the British became, and remained, the most hated race on the new frontier.

Both John and Abel recognized that with fall fast approaching, it was prudent to leave as soon as possible. To prolong the inevitable would only add to the pain and agony. The center of their attention was focused on what they could carry to the waiting ships. Abel placed one item at the top of their carry list — a large iron pot for cooking. Winter clothes and blankets were also important as well as some hand tools including two axes.

Two days after the meeting, Abel, Marie, and Drew struggled to the shore laden with their possessions where they stood in line to board the ship. Abel never told anyone, but he had gone out into their barn and slit the throats of the sturdy Belgian draft horse, the Jersey cow, and two half-grown pigs.

He had planned to burn the cabin until Marie became too hysterical. Marie could not hold back the tears that flowed freely from her dark eyes. Saying good-bye to their home had pushed her close to insanity. Abel was concerned for her.

Abel's family was assigned to a merchant ship then being loaded at the dockside. He recognized Captain Michael Cohen on the bridge of the ship as one of the merchant traders he had done repeated business with over the years. He had told Abel that he was from a small community near the mouth of the Kennebec River in Maine. The Massachusetts General Court offered grants of land to anyone who would migrate to the region. Abel knew that Fort Western had recently been built on the Kennebec at the head of navigation. The friendly Irish ship ,captain told Abel that one of his best friends, Captain James Howard, a Massachusetts provincial officer, was placed in command of the new fort.

John and his family took their place in the line later that afternoon. Abel had promised John that the two families should try to reconnect after they were settled. Penobscot was not so far away from the Kennebec on the Maine coast. John was quieter than usual after the decree. He seemed morbid and crushed for want of an answer to the question he posed over and over: "What civilized nation would do such a ghastly thing?"

Drew remembered how he had said good-bye to Jodi and Pru. It was a solemn parting. He shook hands with Jodi, hoping with all his heart that they would meet again soon. He turned to Pru standing beside her brother crying. So much was suddenly wrong with the world she was too young to understand. Touched by her sorrow, he said, "We have to be on the ship leaving at high tide today. Good-bye, Pru. I'll miss not seeing you every day, and will always remember you. Father has promised that the families will get back together sometime." Suddenly tears formed in his eyes. He did not know that it would be this hard to leave friends and companions that had enriched his young years.

She hugged him and kissed him on the cheek. "Good-bye, my dear friend. I, too, will never forget..." With that she ran rapidly into the barn weeping and gasping for breath.

Drew ran down the path to catch up with his father. He wistfully turned to look back at Pru. She was standing in the barn alone in the large opening waving to him. He returned the wave, choked with emotion.

The British officer took their names, checked them off on his list, and waved them up the ramp to the ship. "As soon as you step on the ship, you are the responsibility of the captain of the vessel."

"That will be an improvement," Abel replied, walking past the arrogant British ensign.

Captain Cohen escorted the LeClair family to the quarters prepared for about fifty families. Several had already preceded them to the lower deck storage area. Each family was allowed about a hundred square feet for the family and their belongings. Abel set up blankets to provide an element of privacy and piled their bags on the outer ring of their assigned space so as to maximize it. They made a pact with their neighbors to look after each other's belongings when members were on the top deck.

Soon after the hold was filled with passengers, the ship pulled anchor and raised sails. Abel left Marie and Drew below and took a place at the port side of the ship for one final view of the cabin and fields filled with crops ready for harvest. He had a sick feeling in his gut. That piece of land and cabin were the product of all his hopes and dreams, but it was all for nothing. To just simply walk away from all his sweat and hard work for the past ten years because he was born in France was pushing him close to the edge of sanity. It would have been easy to deliver a hard blow to the arrogant ensign. It would have given him some release to strike for justice and to dump the ensign in the water. He wondered if the ensign knew how close he came to permanently wearing the smirk he presented to the distraught families.

The ship was under full sail, gaining speed as it silently glided along the western shore of the Minas Basin toward the slender peninsula at Cape Split. Abel located the cabin and the hill behind it, shocked at the ultimate insult taking place. Plumes of dark smoke began to funnel from the cabin. Soon red flames leaped high into the sky as the dry logs slowly turned to charred red coals returning to mother earth from whence they came. Abel could not watch any longer and turned away, sick to his stomach.

The ship picked up a slight breeze out of the east as it plowed from the Basin into the Bay of Fundy. Still sickened by events, Abel made one final glimpse behind the ship. Scattered all over the landscape he could see flames reaching high into the sky consuming cabins, barns, and field crops. The entire region was soon blanketed in black smoke.

The last thing he witnessed at Acadia was another unnecessary outrage the city of Grand Pre was burning! The smoke remained visible from miles out into the bay. The victorious British had transformed Acadia forever. Within a short period of time, no one would ever know how strong, determined men and women had converted a wilderness into a peaceful, productive community. Acadia had experienced deaths and births and had become the place where dreams were fulfilled. It was as close to becoming a Garden of Eden as any other place on this earth, and now..., now it was ruthlessly being destroyed to fulfill the wishes of tyrants.

Abel plucked a tear from his left eye, turning to go below. He had just witnessed the death of paradise, and what angered him the most was that no one would ever know the full potential of what might have been... and nobody was ever held responsible for the inhuman deed.... He found it difficult to understand what had just taken place and cried for justice...

# Chapter Five

The second day of their journey south along the eastern coast, Captain Cohen had promised to insert Abel and his family at a small settlement at the mouth of the Kennebec River. The Captain told Abel that there was a storage facility ashore for supplies destined for Fort Western and Fort Halifax several miles up the Kennebec. At the settlement there was a trading post capable of supplying all of their immediate needs; also, he could apply for a grant of land where he planned to build a dwelling. The trader would facilitate the transfer of free land authorized by the Massachusetts General Court to immigrants.

The question of British rule of the area was mentioned by Captain Cohen who had lived in the colonies since he was a lad the same age as Drew. Abel had thought about it enough that he was willing to take a chance. "When I first came to the New World as a French Marine, I had contact with British authorities in several of the colonies. They were little different from those who banished me and my family from Acadia. I disliked them then, and I detest them even more now. However, colonists who have braved the Atlantic crossing for a new beginning in this land with the opportunity to own land they labor on are a different kind of people." Abel had given the statement a lot of thought. "I trust the men and women with the pioneering spirit more than I hate the Crown and all it stands for. You, Captain Cohen, are a good example of that kind of spirit. Free men can climb any mountain. As difficult as it was to leave my land on the shores of the Basin, I would have eventually thrown off the yoke of control and submission the British in Canada are imposing on their subjects."

Captain Cohen nodded his head. "Aye, Abel, but ye may find the same thing in Maine. I have not experienced any such thing. My roots are in Ireland, but my heart and soul are here in the colonies. There's a difference you can feel. We're much more independent and freer to express our opinions than those across the waters. My main loyalty is to the Colonies, not to Great Britain."

"You've just made my case, Captain," Abel exclaimed. "I predict that the independent, hard-working people who have to risk their all to settle here on the frontier will rise up one day and revolt against the Crown if Parliament restricts their ability to govern themselves and to live as free people. I'm betting on the people, not the governing authorities. If I'm wrong, then we'll have to take our lumps when that time comes."

"Bravo, Abel," the wise Captain Cohen exclaimed and then warned his friend. "You expressed sentiments that are widespread throughout the Colonies. The people who have settled in my little community on the banks of the Kennebec have that kind of attitude. They're the most enterprising people I've known. Of course, some are scoundrels, but for the most part, they're people you can trust when the going gets tough. There's a strong bond of belonging that's hard to define, but you can feel it. Mutual sacrifice binds them together into a brotherhood. Having said that, Abel, do not be deceived. The frontier is a blaze of terror. The French and their allies, the tenacious Abenaki, have been unleashed on the frontier as never before. You'll have to dispel the people's natural fear and distrust of the French. They are our main enemy and their threat to our homes and lives are real. The French have been able to gain ground on the Ohio and have been successful in holding Fort Carillon and Crown Point on Lake Champlain. They are now stronger than the British forces sent to protect the Colonies. Our militia groups do the best they can, but they are severely limited in funds and equipment. Forts Western and Halifax on the Kennebec have helped by providing a place of sanctuary from the marauding bands of Indians."

Abel listened carefully to the Captain. "I did not think it was that bad in Maine."

"Well, the frontier has gained a few more settlers even as the threats have increased. Keep that in mind in selecting a piece of land. Do not venture too far from either fort and stay as close to the river as possible. You'll find it invaluable in receiving things and shipping out timber, firewood, or crops for trade. The river is a road that can lead you to any place in the world."

A week had passed since Abel and his family disembarked onto a dock at the mouth of the Kennebec River. Three other families followed them ashore, yet within three days they had separated and gone their separate ways somewhere in the vast unsettled interior of the Maine wilderness. Abel was pleased by his reception to the area. The factor at the warehouse was anxious to greet newcomers. He looked askance at Marie and was skeptical about having an Indian wife in the region where the mortal threat was from the dreaded Abenaki. After hearing the story of their marriage and of her devotion to her family, the factor told Abel he was a fortunate man. The lovely Delaware maiden with the soft, melodious voice had won his respect and admiration. Abel knew that it was just a question of time.

Thousands of acres were available for those hardy souls with the courage to establish roots in their own piece of land. Forty acre tracts were offered to homesteaders free of charge. All they had to do was build a suitable residence and commence to clear the land for crops for a period of five years. Abel and Marie were willing to start their lives all over again. They really had no other choice except to return to France, which would have been an ordeal greater than carving a home out of the wilderness. There was no more land available in France.

Marie and Drew stayed at the warehouse which also acted as an inn for transients. Abel was curious to look at what was available inland. The factor's son, Loni Jackson, and Abel started upriver in a small sailboat skiff armed with muskets and food for a couple of days. They stayed in midstream for several miles until they came to a large body of fresh water called Merrymeeting Bay. Loni, a slender twenty-year-old young man with red hair and a pleasant demeanor pointed out that they could continue up the river on either side of a large land mass at the northeastern corner of the Bay called Swan Island. There was a scattering of homes all along the river and several places where ships were being constructed. Loni guided the little craft to the right of Swan Island continuing up the river at a pace he would have been pressed to match walking on the shore. They soon came to a large shipbuilding operation with two sawmills on the banks of the river at the junction of a small stream that poured into the Kennebec.

Loni pointed to the site as they glided by, "That's the Colburn Boatyard. It's the largest ship-building facility north of Falmouth and Portsmouth. Mr. Colburn built this sailboat for my father."

"Most of the homes here are constructed of lumber instead of logs. The land is blessed with majestic white pine and hemlock trees with a scattering of oak, beech, birch and maple hardwood trees," Abel replied, impressed with the large tracts of timberland as far as the eye could see.

"Lumber and masts are sold for goods shipped from England where timber is scarce," Loni told him a few miles north of Coburn's boatyard, pulling the skiff into a small cove on the west side of the river. "This is the tract my father wanted me to show you. We think it's one of the best locations on the river."

Abel stepped out of the boat onto shore, pulling it further onto the sandy coastline. He stood on the bank and looked around carefully with his musket cradled in his arms. He saw the towering pine, hemlock and spruce trees along the shore. North of the small cove was a patch of meadow grass in a marshy area slightly affected by the high and low tides of the Atlantic Ocean. He nodded in approval of the several acres of hay just waiting for harvest. "How big is the tract, Loni?"

"It's a rectangular parcel with about eight hundred feet on the riverside. It extends due west from the banks of the river about twenty-seven hundred feet. Like most of the free grants it has about forty acres. My father and Mr. Coburn have had it surveyed with marks on trees at all four corners. That's true of all the tracts located on either side of the river."

They secured the skiff to an alder tree hanging out into the water and walked into the interior of the tract. The level flood plain was relatively free of rocks or granite outcrops. Along the northern boundary close to the western corner was an area of sheer granite cliffs covering a few acres. Abel climbed to the top and paused to look around. The view to the south and east was excellent, even though it was filled with green tree tops and a scattering of hardwoods just beginning to show their fall colors. The panorama gave Abel a feeling of freedom and solace. A soft breeze caressed their faces. They could smell the pungent odor of spruce and fir carried by the prevailing westerly winds. Abel experienced peace and tranquility standing on the towering granite outcrop.

Loni studied his partner for a few minutes. "You like it, don't you, Abel?"

Abel turned to his new friend and smiled. "I think this one will do, Loni. We left a log cabin behind in Acadia. For this location, I'd really like to have a house built out of lumber. Would it be possible to obtain lumber?"

"Mr. Coburn is an easy man to deal with. I'm sure you could work out an arrangement with him. He always is in need of logs which you can easily harvest on your own tract here," Loni suggested.

"That settles it then. Let's head back and close the deal."

"Why don't we take a little longer and eat something? That way the tide will be running out and it will carry us back home quicker than we came north," Loni suggested.

They sat on the bank of the tract and ate pemmican prepared by Loni's father. It was delicious and nourishing, containing blueberries, chestnuts, dried venison, corn meal and molasses. Abel had learned to enjoy the staple food of the native Indians when he served in the French Marines.

On their return trip, Abel was relatively quiet. His head was full of thoughts and plans he was anxious to share with Marie and Drew. This land had a different feel than Acadia where traditionally settlers were content to spend their time "getting by." As long as adequate food and fuel were available, nothing more was expected or desired. Here on the Kennebec, Abel felt an energy totally lacking in Acadia. Resourcefulness and self-reliance bolstered a desire to improve and expand a person's potential. Hope permeated the area; no one stood still by design.

That night, Abel and Marie sat at a table in the tavern with pen and ink, designing a single story house with a large center chimney and a high pitched roof to shed the heavy snows that are normal in the region. That would accommodate two small bedrooms on a second story at each end of the center chimney. They had visited a home nearby with a similar layout. That made it possible for every room to have a fireplace, including the large kitchen one for baking and cooking as well as heat.

The central chimney had several advantages. The fireplaces in rooms at each end of the house formed a square with the central fireplace in the kitchen, creating a large area in the center for smoking meats and fish so that they could be stored for a longer period of time. The sturdy construction could always be used, when not smoking meats, as a secure place to hide in case of an attack by a raiding party of French and Abenaki Indians.

To keep costs down, Abel suggested they could initially start with a minimum of glass windows. Glass and metal hardware were expensive. It had to be purchased from traders shipping it from England. The Colonies were not allowed to manufacture items for their own use. Even cotton from the colonies in the south had to be shipped to England where it was manufactured into linens and clothing, and then sent back to the Colonies for sale at a profit.

Most of the people in the region were of Scotch-Irish ancestry. They had brought with them their traditional work ethics and skills in working with wood, granite, or bricks, which they made nearby. It was one of the manufactured products that could not be transported across the ocean at a profit. Most of the lumber-built homes were placed on granite foundations, which were usually located close by the building site.

A few days after his trip upriver with Loni, Abel signed with Marie for the forty-acre parcel of land on the western shore of the Kennebec River. Abel and Drew both took jobs at the Coburn Boatyard to earn money to pay for the construction of their home as they had planned it. Between the two of them, they earned fifteen schillings per day. The men who were building their home cost about thirty schillings per day, so Abel promised Mr. Coburn to work all winter to pay for the construction while he and Marie temporarily took up residence in a tent pitched behind their house. As soon as the cellar and foundation were completed, they could move to the improved shelter in severe weather. Once the root cellar and foundation were completed, they concentrated on a small barn or shed for temporary living quarters.

There was always a cautious state of anticipation within the frontier community. Experience taught the settlers that terror from the wilderness came when least expected. That condition of wariness was relaxed in the wintertime when the snow was deep and travel in the forest was exhausting. The snow also left a trail for tracking the attackers. Aside from the Abenaki, winter was the primary enemy. Winter in the north woods of Maine could be a brutal adversary to those who were unprepared for its powerful impact.

The first snow had come late in November. By that time, the LeClair home had been framed and the roof was completed with cedar shingles from their own cedar trees in a small swamp at the extreme western end of their forty acres. They anticipated having the house completed by springtime. Bricks were obtained from a local Scotch mason who produced them from moist clay that was heated to a high temperature in wood-fired kilns. The demand for his bricks exceeded his ability to produce them, so he took orders, having every customer take their turn. Bricks for the LeClair chimneys were not available until October. Abel had the man building the fireplaces to concentrate on the main kitchen fireplace so that they could use a portion of the house for the winter. The rest could wait until warmer weather in the spring.

One day, Abel and Drew plodded through the packed snow on a path beside the river leading to their home from the boatyard. They were living temporarily in the one room shed. Abel felt a thrill of pride run through him when he first saw the new home with a curl of wood smoke wafting from the large chimney in the kitchen. Drew pointed to a small sailboat tied up at the floating dock father and son had constructed earlier that fall. They rushed to see who was at the house, when Marie opened the door and hailed them, "We have some unexpected guests — our friends John, Rosalee, and Prudence."

# Chapter Six

It was a poignant reunion of friends who had experienced the same shameful treatment from the British in Nova Scotia. John looked tired and beaten. Abel had never seen him so dejected. When asked where he had been after leaving Acadia, John told them he and his family had tried to assimilate into the frontier area around Penobscot Bay where there had been a strong French influence for generations. Essentially, they were just not happy there. Many of the French families had left the region for Louisiana. Those who remained were contemplating that same move. John told them that he and his family planned to catch a ship stopping at the familiar warehouse location at the mouth of the Kennebec River the next day. They too were going to a warmer climate on that boat. The warehouse factor that had been so helpful to Abel and the family graciously let John take his sailboat to meet with his friends, the LeClairs.

"I'm sorry to hear that, John. I was looking forward to seeing you soon. We've been busy trying to beat old man winter. Why don't you try your luck here on the Kennebec? Forty acres are available for the asking up the river from here towards Fort Western. Now that we've got the shell for the house completed, we'd be glad to share our primitive conditions with you. Perhaps this place is like Penobscot, but make no mistakes about the people. They first and foremost consider themselves as colonists, then English or Irish. The French that have been terrorizing the frontier with their Abenaki allies are despised and feared, yet, I've experienced no prejudice towards my nationality here. To be honest, I'm thinking more and more like an American. What do you think, John?"

John looked at his wife for some response. He noted a small sigh of relief in her smile. "The warm weather in Louisiana had appealed to us. It would be nice to have old friends for neighbors instead of strangers. Having to leave Acadia the way we did has ignited a strong hatred of the British that is almost overpowering."

"Direct that at the Crown and Parliament, not at the Colonists, who are settlers just like us," Abel admonished his friend. "We'd be happy to help you settle in. The winter will be difficult, but by spring you and Rosalee will be full of enthusiasm. The river is teeming with codfish, lobsters and salmon. The natives have fished the rivers and collected wild rice on the bay for centuries."

John looked again at his wife. There was some hesitation in her heart. Finally, she nodded to her husband with tears filling her eyes. "We'll accept your generous offer, John and Marie. How fortunate we are to have friends like you. I've been frightened for my family before we stopped by for a visit. Your logic is convincing, Abel." Rosalee gave a sigh of relief.

"You sound like the authoritative officer your men always called you," Abel remarked.

"Sometimes I miss the camaraderie that was a big part of the military," John replied with a grin.

While the adults were conversing, Drew poured Prudence a hot cup of tea and one for himself. They sat at a counter on the opposite side of the kitchen so that they could talk. "Would you like an apple pie, Pru? We just got a supply from an orchard downstream a ways. Mother bakes a big batch of them ahead. Father and I take a couple each when we go to work at the boatyard."

"I'd like that, Drew. I'm hungry. Jodi got married the day we left Acadia. He's gone on to Louisiana. His wife's family had already settled there."

"Do you miss Jodi?"

"Sure, but Papa plans to follow in his footsteps," she replied, savoring the baked apple pie covered with a heavy crust of dough.

Drew had been listening to the adults and quickly corrected her assertion. "I just heard your father agree to stay with us while looking for a suitable piece of land here on the Kennebec. I'm glad. I'd hate to think of you being far away down south."

"Then Papa has changed his mind again," Pru confided to Drew in a partial whisper. "He's been so depressed lately, and has been drinking more hard cider. Your father will be a good influence on him. I didn't want to go to Louisiana. I really miss our reading and writing sessions in your mother's kitchen. Do you still study?"

"Mother insists, especially since we're building a new life here in Maine. If we're to be accepted by the community we should be able to read and write so as to communicate properly with people," Drew told her. "Even on days that I work eight hours in the sawmill, she takes time during and after supper to continue the lessons."

"What do you do at the sawmill, Drew?"

"I help to pile the boards when they have logs to saw. I sort them by species into pine, hemlock, spruce, cedar, or hardwoods. Some of the boards are heavy, but I'm learning how to handle them. I make several schillings a day," he proudly announced. "I want to help pay for the house. When that is done, I'm going to save for a rifled carbine musket like my father has."

"You've grown older looking, Drew. When you left Acadia, I was afraid I would never see you again," she said in a whisper.

"It looks like we'll see a lot of each other this winter, Pru. Maybe I'll end up making a pest of myself when you see me every day," he laughed, putting another log on the fire.

Drew had grown a little taller and had filled out his relatively thin physique since Pru had last seen him. They could always laugh with each other. How nice it was, she thought. He was a gentle person like his father and mother. He was darker of complexion than other young men, and he had the high cheek bones and dark eyes like his Delaware mother. She thought he was a very handsome-looking young man and was proud to be his friend.

41

That winter of 1755-56 the two families shared the home generously offered by the LeClair family. The two bedrooms upstairs still did not have a usable fireplace, but they were kept warm with heavy blankets and several bear and moose robes. It was nice to hear laughter and to feel the camaraderie that existed between the two families. It was not long before the sorrows of Acadia were pushed from their consciousness, replaced by a newfound joy of creating a new home and a new life on the frontier that was well-served by the river.

Goods from all over the globe were eventually available to the inhabitants along the waterway. Glass, metal products, and porcelain were offered for sale by merchant traders who plied the eastern seaboard. It was a profitable trade, and many of the ships were made along the banks of the Kennebec and the Penobscot Rivers. The goods most prized were the delicacies from the tropical islands in the Caribbean — oranges, bananas, rum, molasses, sugar, rice, and coffee, a beverage that was gaining in popularity in the colonies. It was replacing tea in many homes when it was available. One ship came to offer a new beverage called cocoa, a fine flour made from the cocoa bean. It soon became a favorite with Drew and his mother. He never got enough of it.

Life on the frontier had its moments of joy and simple satisfaction, creating something tangible from the raw land. Survival demanded vigilance that was never allowed to falter. The vast frontier from Maine west to the Hudson River was controlled by small roving bands of Abenaki Indians, usually controlled by French officers and/or Jesuit priests, who were looking for opportunities to strike settlers in isolated hamlets creating terror and fear. One by one the brave settlers who took the chance to venture inland were butchered and tortured in front of their families. Their reign of terror had few equals in the world. The savagery came unexpectedly from the forest with a ferocity few survived, and those who did survive were marked forever by the obscene brutality they had witnessed.

To help alleviate this fear of the unknown, two forts were built on the Kennebec: Fort Western a few miles north of the LeClair home at the head of navigation on the Kennebec, and Fort Halifax, nine miles farther north on the river. The

Kennebec had been the Indian's main pathway to Canada. Generations of Penobscots, Micmacs, and Abenaki had traveled the area and they were reluctant to release their prior claim to the land.

The pattern of attacks continued as usual, but the Abenaki seemed interested in taking hostages to be ransomed for high prices. It soon became a very lucrative business for them. They selected those people who were physically strong enough to withstand the long trip to their Indian encampment, known as Odanak, located on the convergence of the Saint Francis and the Saint Lawrence Rivers in Canada.

A year after John and Rosalee visited Abel and Marie, the Boisvert's home was completed with several acres of land cleared for crops. John also took a job at the boatyard with Mr. Coburn as a joiner. He became a skilled craftsman and earned good wages for his labor. Abel and Drew continued to work at the sawmill or in the forest cutting logs.

Occasionally, Drew took a job offered by Mr. Jackson, the factor of the large warehouse at the mouth of the river, to help his son, Loni, sail two small boats up to Fort Western with supplies. Quite often the boats drew hostile fire from the shore. The boat Loni was sailing was equipped with a small swivel cannon mounted next to the tiller. It was loaded with rocks, nails and jagged pieces of molten lead with a maximum charge of gunpowder. It was capable of reaching past the distance to the shore and usually scattered the Indians with its deadly projectiles which tore gaping wounds in flesh.

Whenever Drew agreed to take one of the boats to Fort Western, Abel insisted that he take his rifled musket carbine and a pistol with him. Drew turned out to be an excellent marksman for his age. His father had drilled him so that he could load, aim, and fire three shots a minute. Abel boasted that, as a French Marine, he was expected to shoot four rounds a minute and hit a six inch target a hundred feet away.

One day after they had filled the boats with the cargo for the fort, Loni and Drew began their drive north as the incoming tide neutralized some of the force of the mighty Penobscot's flow toward the Atlantic. The fort was primarily supplied by schooners from Boston about four times a year. It took about three hours to travel to the fort with the small sails. They unloaded the boats onto the large dock and ate in the mess hall located in the large barracks building inside the stockade. The fort was garrisoned by fifteen Massachusetts Provincial troops commanded by Captain James Howard. Its main armament was a four inch cannon and several swivel guns mounted in blockhouses at the four corners of the palisade.

Drew was on the starboard side of the sailboat on their return trip from the fort traveling in the center of the river when they experienced musket fire from the western shore. One of the lead bullets hit the upper edge of the wooden gunwale, shattering it. Drew cried out in pain when wooden splinters penetrated his right arm.

Loni saw what was happening, lowered the sail, and leaped to the rear of the boat to use the swivel gun. He always carried a small pistol with the pan primed with gunpowder which he emptied into the swivel gun's fire hole and then turned the pistol over the hole pulling the trigger. Sparks flew from the flint igniting the small cannon. A fraction of a second later, the gun belched smoke and flame from the stubby barrel toward the location where Loni saw smoke puffs from muskets. His aim was true. They heard a high pitched scream from the alder thicket on the shore.

Drew had already drawn his carbine in case he saw a target of opportunity. He saw movement near the base of the alder trees and fired his weapon at the movement. The musket was loaded with two lead bullets on top of each other. Another loud yelp echoed through the stillness of the forest.

"How badly are you hit, Drew?" Loni asked, quickly reloading the swivel gun.

Drew's arm was covered with blood. "Let's get out of here, Loni. I'm all right. The gunwale saved my life," he replied, reloading the carbine.

The first house they came to was that of John Boisvert. They both agreed that they should stop to check on the family and to alert them to the presence of Indians on their side of the river. Drew guided the boat up to the small floating dock John had built, jumping with carbine in hand onto it to secure the sailboat to a hitching post. The two then ran to the house yelling if anyone was at home. Drew saw a thin trickle of smoke wafting from the chimney, a good sign! The front door was immediately yanked open to let them in. They were met by a frantic and excited Prudence.

"Thank God you're here," she exclaimed, closing and bolting the door behind them.

"What's wrong, Pru?" Drew asked. "We just ran into Indians a short distance from here."

"Yes, we know about them. Mother and I were splitting and piling wood behind the house when mother spotted an Indian at the edge of their field opening. She screamed for us to run to the house and barricade the doors... Mother knows how to shoot my father's musket, so we went upstairs to try and locate them from a better vantage point..." she was crying and shaking all over. She told them that one of the Indians had come close to the house in the field and must have seen them in the upstairs window. He had fired, wounding Rosalee. "Mother's still upstairs lying on the bed..." Pru screamed hysterically.

Loni and Drew ran up the stairs to check on her. They found her on the bed in the room with the broken glass. She had been hit on her thigh. It had bled a lot and apparently missed any bones, for she could move her leg without a lot of pain. She was lucky and was also very angry.

"I've seen a lot of wounds in my lifetime, and this one is not serious," she tried to calm the two young men. "I've wrapped it in clean linen with a little gunpowder," she laid down on the bed exhausted. "Thank God Prudence was able to shoot the musket. We saw one of the Indians fall in the grass."

Drew looked at Loni. "Should we go out there to see if the body is still there?"

"No, I suggest that we stay put until Mr. Boisvert returns from work at the boatyard," Loni added. "We should warn him to approach the house with caution."

Drew turned to Prudence who was looking at the blood dripping down over his hand. She was alarmed and asked, "What happened, Drew?"

"It's nothing really, Pru," he replied. "One of the Indians shot at me in the boat. A splinter jabbed me in the arm. It's bleeding a little, that's all."

"Let me look at it," she demanded. "You'll have to take off your shirt. The sleeve is full of blood." She ran downstairs to get a clean cloth and a pan of warm water to clean the wound.

"You go downstairs with Prudence, Drew. I'll stay up here and keep a lookout from the roof. What time does your husband usually get home from work, Mrs. Boisvert?" Loni inquired.

"He's due any minute, Loni. You should shoot to warn him to be careful."

Loni climbed up the ladder to the roof trap door and stepped out onto the roof to fire his musket into the air. A few seconds later, he heard John hail him from the path beside the river. John ran into the house worried that something had happened.

Ten minutes later, they were all sitting around the kitchen table beside the fireplace waiting for the water to boil for hot tea. Pru had already dressed Drew's open wound with clean linen and insisted that he put one of her father's shirts on.

John was proud of his wife and Prudence. "This is our first encounter with what is commonplace on the frontier today. In time, this threat will disappear, but for now, it's a challenge that cannot last a lifetime. Vigilance must be a way of life, and we must look after each other the way our two young friends have shown," he sighed, resigned to the risk.

Pru was concerned for Drew. He looked tired and detached. He was still a young boy, yet he had conducted himself like a grown man. She knew that he was eleven years old, a year younger than her. He was in that awkward adolescent stage that boys often go through. She served him his tea and took a seat beside him. She deftly plucked a strand of hair from his face and placed her hand on his forehead, "Are you feeling all right, Drew?" she asked.

Suddenly he felt a little dizzy and slumped over on the table spilling his tin of tea. John and Loni jumped to his side. They picked his limp body up and laid him on the small cot near the fireplace. To everyone's surprise, the clean shirt Pru had given him was covered with blood on his right side. Closer examination revealed another wound on his body. A bullet, possibly the same one that had splintered the gunwale, had entered the fleshy portion of his side just below his ribs. His loss of blood made him delirious and very weak.

# Chapter Seven

Three years Later – Fall, 1760

Drew stood on the port side of the sleek schooner sailing north on the Atlantic seaboard under full sail. Majestic Mount Agamenticus rose from the coastal plain dominating the skylight. It had been a guiding landmark for generations of mariners. To Drew, it meant that home was not far away. The ship sliced through the water with ease. Its shallow draft allowed the vessel to travel in waters closer to shore unsuitable for heavier freighters. It was an important factor in case the nimble craft needed to evade heavier armed ships.

The schooner had just delivered supplies at the Market Dock in Portsmouth, New Hampshire, and was enroute to the Kennebec River further north on the Maine coast. They had a shipment of molasses, nails, and glass for Fort Western. Drew had signed on as a deck hand for as long as he wanted to serve. The experience had opened his eyes to a part of the world he would normally never visit. The ship made three separate trips to the Caribbean ports of Puerto Rico, Santa Domingo, and Cuba where they loaded the ship to capacity with rum, molasses, sugar, and a large variety of fruits such as bananas and oranges. They distributed their cargo to the British colonies along the eastern seaboard. Boston and Portsmouth were two important destinations for products from the Caribbean. They often loaded the sloop with lumber for their return trip south.

Drew's visit home during the three years he served on the schooner were infrequent. The Captain of the ship went where he could make the most profit, but he had taken a liking to the young Drew and made an effort to stop at the Kennebec every ten months or so for Drew to have a short visit at home. Drew thought often about the incident that had caused him to faint from loss of blood at Pru's home. John had forced him to drink all the liquids he could to replenish the lost blood. It had embarrassed him in front of Pru. John and Loni had taken him home to his parents who had been worried.

The experience on board the small craft had helped him to make the adjustment from an adolescent boy to a young man prepared to take on the world. He had gained a few pounds and had grown several inches taller. The grueling routine on the sailing ship demanded alertness and the ability to work and act as an integral part of a team that made the ship function. At times when the sea was rough and the winds howled through the rigging, a misstep could spell disaster. With three years under the masts he had physically matured beyond his youthful years. He had grown into a strong man very much like his father.

Settlements along the Kennebec were still subjected to the wrath of the French and Indians on the frontier. There was much talk on the schooner about the war taking place. They picked up information at every port they entered. Therefore, they were as well informed as anyone in the colonies. The British seemed to be gaining on the battlefields. Ever since the massive loss of life by British General Braddock at Fort Duquesne on the Ohio River, and by the incompetent General Abercrombie at Fort Carillon at the base of Lake Champlain, the British had increased their commitment to the struggle for a continent. Their forces grew in strength and numbers while the French forces slowly declined.

Those lonely settlers on the frontier from the Ohio to the Penobscot in Maine were the object of large numbers of French troops and their Indian allies intent on their destruction. Though the French were losing battle after battle, their intense pressure on the frontier showed no sign of lessening. Everywhere the schooner went, the main topic of conversation was about the inflamed frontier. Ultimately in 1759 the French were decisively defeated on the Plains of Abraham at Quebec. The last remaining stronghold of French influence was at

Montreal, where their defeat was only a question of time. The British had gained control over those portions of the hemisphere once controlled by Spain, the Dutch, and now France. Britannia now ruled North America.

Drew watched the prominent mountain peak rise above the coastal plain of southern Maine. Located slightly north of the entrance to Portsmouth, New Hampshire, harbor, it had been a familiar landmark for generations of sailors. Drew was coming home, and his heart was pounding with excitement. The familiar Isles of Shoals and the sunlit peak of Mount Agamenticus announced that it would not be long before the sleek schooner turned into the calmer waters at the mouth of the Kennebec River. The owner of the schooner, Captain Jones, stood beside Drew, understanding how the young man felt. He was a gentle man who wore the mantel of authority with grace. His reputation as an honest man had contributed to his financial success as a merchant seaman.

"Well, Drew, you'll soon be able to see the Kennebec. Your absence from home at this crucial time in your life will always be remembered. I'll be glad to reach Machias after we drop you off at the warehouse at the mouth of the Kennebec."

"My mother and father will be surprised, that's for sure, Sir. The open sea and sun have been a new experience for me. My mother will be the first to see how I've tanned these past months. I'll never forget the times I was mortally scared when the waves were breaking over the schooner," Drew excitedly recalled.

Captain Jones smiled at his youngest sailor. "You've been a good hand, Drew. Anytime you're looking for a job at sea, I'll be glad to take you on."

"Thank you, Sir. My father is going to be envious when he sees my new carbine with a rifled barrel. Those craftsmen in Pennsylvania did a beautiful job on the weapon."

"Ah, and its price is right. I've traded a lot with the man who buys the rifles from craftsmen back in the hills. It's illegal to manufacture or to purchase them, but the craftsmanship is worth the risk. We'll be reaching the Kennebec by nightfall. I plan to stay overnight with my old friend of many years, Mudge Jackson," Captain Jones said.

The Captain's estimate was perfect. Just as the sun began to set, the schooner was being secured to Jackson's dock. Drew was offered the use of Jackson's sailboat for the trip home up the river. There was a large harvest moon already lifting from the eastern horizon to help guide his path to home. A slight breeze from the northeast filled the sail so that with the incoming tide, and the wind, Drew was able to develop a zig-zag pattern that propelled the small craft at a fast pace over the dark water.

The full moon lit his path up the river. Three hours later, Drew lowered the sail and lightly slid into his father's dock. He anxiously secured the boat and ran to the front door and knocked. His father asked, "Who goes there?"

"It's me, Father," knowing that he would never open the door at night to a stranger after dark.

His mother opened the door and wrapped her arms around her son. "Our wandering son has returned to us safe and sound. Thank God," she exclaimed with tears of joy running down her cheeks.

Drew glanced over her shoulder at his father with a serious look on his face. He embraced Drew. "Your mother has said it right, thank God, my son."

John and Pru were also gathered around the fire in the kitchen. Pru left her chair and hugged him. There was a somber air in the room. "Hi, Mr. Boisvert. Is something wrong?" he asked, still holding Pru.

"You came at a sad time, Drew. We just buried my mother. She was killed by Abenaki who came out of the forest to kill and to destroy," Pru told him with fear and apprehension still in her eyes.

John sat with his head cradled in both hands filled with uncontrollable grief. Drew released Pru and placed a comforting hand on John's shoulder. "I'm so sorry for both of you. I brought several newspapers I collected at different ports along the coast. They all write about the explosion of violence on the frontier. There isn't any solution in sight until the French relinquish the claims to which they stubbornly cling. The Ohio is ablaze with conflict. Not just from Indians but from white criminals who kill and steal just as viciously as the natives. I was hoping I'd find things different here on the Kennebec."

Pru took a seat beside her father and clasped her arms around his shoulders. Drew sat next to his mother, taking her hand in his. She smiled bravely. "Let me get you something to eat, son."

"A hot cup of tea with one of your apple pies, if you have any, would be great, Mother," he answered, sobered by the tragedy he had come home to. He watched Pru and her father. It was hard to believe that the lovely Rosalee Boisvert was dead in the prime of her life!

His father told Drew that Rosalee and Prudence were working in the garden gathering crops for storage when a band of four Indians surprised them. Rosalee was immediately attacked and brutishly raped several times in front of Pru. The band was being pursued by a group of soldiers from Fort Western who arrived on the scene when Rosalee was being violated. They quickly killed her with a tomahawk to her skull and fled. The soldiers had saved Pru from the same experience, and were able to kill all four of the offenders.

That evening, after John and Pru reluctantly settled into quest rooms in the house, Drew retired to the familiar room on the west side of the house where he was able to watch the moon hang over the distant hills where the sun set every evening. He had often watched it sink from view. Traditionally the nights were relatively safe from Indian attacks. They believed that their spirits would be lost in the darkness if they were killed in combat at night. It was a time throughout the frontier when settlers could reflect inward with their normal safety precautions relaxed. It was a daily reprieve from the very real pressure of anticipation.

Drew thought about what his father had told him earlier that evening. British General Amherst had successfully attacked and captured the massive fortress at Louisbourg. Now that same general was accepting the surrender of French forces at Montreal. The French had been driven from the hemisphere! His father laments that whenever he puts down roots the British show their ugly head. Hatred of the British still lingered in his heart. Was the LeClair family now going to be removed from the Kennebec???

Abel confided to his son that evening that he would resist any attempt by the Crown to solicit any oath of allegiance to the Crown or to evict him from the land he had worked so hard to develop. His allegiance was to the land opened up by the colonists not to the greedy Crown!

"But where would you go, Father?" Drew asked. "The whole coast to Florida is under British control."

Abel shook his head. "Perhaps we'll be lucky, and they'll leave us alone. I pray for that solution. I heard from one of the soldiers at Fort Western that the Bay Colony was advertising for new settlers to come to Maine."

"That's true, Father," Drew said. "Captain Jones is bringing a family of five to the Penobscot region tomorrow morning."

The privacy of his old room was a change from the open hold below decks he and the other sailors used as sleeping quarters on the schooner. He did enjoy the feeling of camaraderie that existed among the crew of the ship, inspired by Captain Jones. Drew had often thought about the possibility of his owning a ship in the future. The sea held a certain fascination for him. For now he had a feeling that he was needed here on the Kennebec waterfront. He fell asleep dreaming about how life had been back in Acadia.

Everyone was up by the time Drew quietly came downstairs to the welcome fire of the kitchen. The fall had a bite to it, and a fire felt good. He helped himself to a heaping bowl of oatmeal sprinkled with a liberal amount of sugar from Cuba. He also took a small fillet of smoked salmon from the platter his mother handed to him. Pru sat with her father on the bench beside the fireplace with a tin cup of tea in her hand. Her eyes were glazed as she stared off into space. It frightened him, and he was no longer as hungry as he had been.

John and his father were talking about all of the crops they had yet to get under cover before snowfall. Squash, potatoes, beets and carrots had been left for last because they were able to withstand a frost if one came earlier than expected. John was not anxious to have Pru stay at the house alone. She had been working part time at Fort Western in the mess hall and laundry facility. Abel asked Drew if he had any specific plans for the day.

Drew announced, "No, Father. Captain Jones left some supplies at the warehouse for the fort. I thought I'd volunteer to help carry some of them up the river. If you have anything for me to do, I'd be glad to help. You know that. That's what I came home for."

His father nodded approval for his grown-up son. "What do you think, John? Drew is capable of taking Pru to the fort where she'll be safe until you've adjusted to your routines without Rosalee. Or, if she wants, she can stay here with us."

Drew looked at Pru over his dish of salmon. She caught his eye and smiled at him. A smile, he thought, that's an improvement! "I'm available to take Pru to the fort. I've got Mr. Jackson's small sailboat tied up at the dock. I'll take my new carbine with me. What do you want to do, Pru?"

She placed her empty cup on the table. "The garrison cook told me he always has a job for me if I want to work. The fort is very busy now with Fort Halifax being opened up. All of the supplies for Halifax are coming through Western," she replied. "Right now I don't know what I want. I think Father will be relieved if I'm safe at the fort. That may be the best thing to do for now."

John was relieved that Drew could take Pru to the fort in the small sailboat that everyone in the neighborhood had borrowed at one time or another. The tide was coming in, so everyone rushed to gather Pru's belongings to take advantage of the inward flow of the river. John warned Drew to hold closer to the east shore. Most of the sightings of Indians lately have been on the western side. Abel helped Drew lift two barrels of smoked codfish he had promised the fort.

Pru accepted Drew's hand boarding the small craft, taking a seat next to his beside the tiller. She was quiet and reflective as they were pulled into midstream by the powerful current. The wind was out of the northwest, helping to propel the small craft heading slightly east of north. Drew turned the boat close to the eastern shore, slowly returning to midstream. He continued that pattern, constantly scanning both sides of the riverbank for anything out of the ordinary.

Pru watched her best friend handle the sail and the tiller with a light touch. He had grown taller and slightly heavier in the past year. The healthy tan made him look older and more mature than his fifteen years. She noted that he was more confident and relaxed than he used to be. Her friend Drew still had the good manners and the same caring, unselfish attitude that had defined him as a little boy. He had carefully loaded and primed his carbine when he first got into the boat, leaning it against the seat next to him. He took his role as protector seriously, conscious of her evaluation of him.

"It's nice being here with you, Pru," he said, breaking the silence. "I feel awful about your mother. Your poor father is devastated. I never dreamed I'd come home to such a loss."

"I'm really concerned for my father. Ever since we left Acadia, he's changed. He's a more bitter man than he used to be. Lately he's more moody and angry when things don't go as he planned. At times I feel as if I was a burden to him," she exclaimed, holding back the tears.

"My God, Pru. If what you say is true, then he's changed from the man I looked up to as a little boy in Acadia. My father always respected him as his superior officer."

They passed an area in the river known as Gardiner after a prominent family that settled on the Kennebec several years ago. The river was deep enough for large ocean vessels to travel up to Fort Western. They had about nine more miles to get to the fort. A large freighter with full sails was coming down the river on their way to England with a full load of white pine mast trees used for the Royal Navy's ships of the line. Some trees were seventy feet tall making them ideal for the largest and most powerful navy in the world.

The Crown had sent surveyors into the colonial forests to mark those large straight white pine trees suitable for masts with a King's arrow. They had found that old growth white pine had little taper and was flexible and straight grained — perfect for the Royal Navy.

Drew had folded a blanket for Pru to sit on beside him. She was quieter than usual on the trip. He understood her need for solitude and moments to reflect. Her sad eyes made him feel helpless that there was nothing he could do to ease her pain. He was resolved to be there when and if she needed him.

The long year he had spent at sea since his last visit home had given him a much greater perception of the world beyond the horizon. That period of his youth had been intoxicating and had expanded his awareness of people and places that he would never have known without taking the job as a deck hand on the schooner. Yet, he was glad to be back home. He had a feeling that he had been away for a longer period of time than he actually had. Home and hearth held precious memories, many of which he shared with Pru sitting silently beside him.

An hour and half later, they could see some of the stockade around Fort Western. Drew asked Pru how long she had been working at the fort.

"I worked most of the summer. I went there once with my father and Mr. Jackson to deliver vegetables. Father knew Captain Howard, the commander of the fort. I was offered a job in the kitchen and laundry facility. I earned some money and had a private room at the fort. The work was hard, but everyone treated me very well," she told him.

Drew aimed the boat for the large shipping dock, throwing a line to a soldier standing by to catch it. Drew helped Pru step out of the boat and turned to unload the two barrels of salt codfish onto the dock. There were several soldiers standing on the dock. One of the men ran to Pru, picking her up and twirling her around.

Drew acted on instinct, kicking the intruder in the groin and hit him with a hard right in the face, giving him a bloody nose. It all happened so fast... Pru screamed hysterically at him, "Stop, Drew, stop it...! This is Corporal Mason... we're engaged to marry...!!

# Chapter Eight

The words Prudence screamed ignited a response that exploded in his mind. It was incredulous... He must have heard wrong... His Pru engaged to another man, a virtual stranger! It was as if he was transported to another world. He felt dizzy and disoriented as if his opponent had risen from the dock, delivering a stunning blow to his head. The pain and shock that accompanied the message coming from his Pru's mouth was more than he could gracefully accept.

All the way up the river, Prudence had been searching for the right words to tell Drew, but images of her mother's death still clouded her reasoning. She had rationally thought that it would be easier to explain when she introduced Drew to her beau, Corporal Joseph Mason. She had misjudged and underrated Drew's feelings for her. The eruption of conflict caught everyone off guard.

Reality and rationality slowly returned to Drew looking down at the man lying on the dock. Pru grasped his right arm to restrain his impulse. "Drew, stop... My God, stop!..." she screamed again, her eyes full of tears.

He angrily pulled away from her grip, hurt and stunned by her betrayal of his feelings for her. He turned to confront Corporal Mason. "I apologize for my actions. I did not know..."

Two soldiers had leaped to hold him. He never felt so alone in his life. He cried out to the two soldiers, "May I see Captain Howard?"

"He's at his headquarters in the building next to the dock," one of the soldiers said, releasing his arm and pointing to a door.

Anxious to leave an embarrassing scene, Drew aimlessly walked towards the door. Captain Howard was waiting for someone to report to him. He had seen the disturbance on the dock. He recognized Drew, greeting him casually. "I noticed you and John Boisvert's daughter arriving at the fort. What happened out there, Drew?"

"I made a fool out of myself, Sir. I beat up on Corporal Mason for no good reason than my surprise that he and Prudence are engaged. She's been a good friend for a long time... I was unaware of their arrangement. I apologize for my actions," Drew openly confessed to the officer who was a good friend to his father.

"Corporal Mason is a good person, Drew. I accept your apology. We all have moments we'd like to forget. Now, I'm glad to see you. Your father has kept me informed of your duty on a sailing ship," Captain Howard said, calmly studying the sturdy young man before him with hat in hand. "I have a favor to ask of you. Would you join a party of men I'm organizing to transport supplies to Fort Halifax? I plan to send shallow draft scows up the river and a convoy of wagons by the road cut between the two forts on the western side of the river. Your father has told me that you're a good shot and are capable of firing three aimed shots a minute. Is that true?"

Drew modestly shook his head, "Perhaps I can beat that time with my new carbine with a rifled barrel. I have it in the sailboat."

"Would you be interested in joining our expedition?"

"I have no immediate plans, Captain. I was going to return the sailboat to the warehouse for Mr. Jackson," Drew said.

"I have two workmen going to the coast. They could return the craft to Jackson for you," Captain suggested.

"That being the case, I agree to your request, Captain. I think I need a change of scene right now."

"I must tell you that the frontier is just as dangerous as ever, Drew. The war is going well for us, but the native uprising is still very active. We have incidents every day as you know with Mrs. Boisvert's tragic death," Captain Howard warned Drew.

Drew understood what the Captain was telling him. "We picked up bits and pieces of information as we traveled north up the coast. I assumed that the French were beaten."

"I recently came from Fort Number Four at Charlestown, New Hampshire, on the Connecticut River. My old friend Captain Phineas Stevens informed me that strikes by the Abenaki from Odanak on the Saint Lawrence are as numerous as ever. Now is no time to relax our guard," Captain Howard stated forcefully.

"If I say yes, would you contact my folks to let them know where I am?" Drew asked.

"I could have the men who take your sailboat deliver a message to your mother and father. We'll be pleased to have you on our team. The wagons on the west bank will give some flank protection to the scows and barges. I'd like you to take your carbine and act as a flanker for the wagons. A Lieutenant William Jellison will be in command of the operation. He'll be your immediate superior. Does that sound okay?"

"Every job has its boss," Drew smiled. "I like working as part of a team. Captain Jones ran a tight ship, and I got along just fine taking orders."

"Captain Jones is one of the best. You were lucky to have him introduce you to the work force as an important player. He had some nice things to say about you, young man," Captain Howard smiled at him.

"I learned a lot with him. I hope I've grown some in the process," Drew quickly added.

"The scows and wagons are on their way down from Halifax," Captain Howard told him. "As soon as they arrive, every available man will help to load the scows and wagons from the warehouse. The trip can be made in half to three quarters of a day. Why don't you have a cup of hot tea while you're waiting? Once you arrive at Halifax they'll put you up in their barracks for the night. Then you can return as you wish. You've got a busy couple of days ahead of you, Drew. Welcome aboard."

Drew left the commander's quarters to retrieve his carbine and a heavy doeskin hunting jacket his mother had made for him. Reluctant to run into Pru or Corporal Mason, he went into

59

the mess hall and helped himself to a hot cup of tea and a piece of bread with molasses, taking a seat in the corner of the room to be as inconspicuous as possible.

Pru had silently watched him take a seat near the large fireplace, noting the sad look on his face. She quickly went to sit opposite from him. "I wanted to tell you, Drew. I really did. I wanted you to be happy for me. Can you do that for me, Drew?" she asked in a wavering voice.

He looked at her red swollen eyes, "If you had asked that of me, I would have questioned your judgment in acting so quickly. I would have wanted the best for my friend. I came back from the sea with every intention of seeing more of you. Remember, when we were younger in Acadia, we had planned a future together. I was prepared, even anxious, to follow through on our fantasies. Perhaps both of us were too young and inexperienced to make decisions that last a lifetime. Now that I know it's not meant to be, I'm saddened by the reality. However, I could never wish you unhappiness. If your heart tells you that this is what you want, then you and Joseph have my blessings. I wanted more and was working hard to be worthy of you, Pru." He got up from the table and slowly walked out to the loading dock. He was too proud to let her see how badly he was affected by her decision.

An hour later, the scows pushed off the dock for their slow movement up the Kennebec. Six supply wagons pulled out onto the supply road built on the west bank of the river. Drew was given the task of acting as a scout on the western flank of the convoy about a hundred yards into the forest. The column was commanded by a Lieutenant William Jellison who rode his horse next to the lead wagon. He was a short chunky man with years of experience in Nova Scotia. A soldier was at the point on the road and one at the rear of the column. A third soldier was riding in the lead wagon.

Drew was glad to be alone with his thoughts dominated by Pru. She came out of the building to wave good-bye to him. He had turned his back on her to check the flint and prime of his carbine. He was entering enemy territory and scolded himself to be alert, for he was responsible for the safety of the wagons. His father had frequently stressed that a man took responsibility seriously. It was a virtuous gift that Captain Jones had encouraged on his schooner.

Two miles out from Fort Western, Drew climbed a knoll that overlooked the road beside the river and into an old burned area filled with raspberry bushes and grey birch saplings sprouting up from the blackened earth. He saw a movement ahead that looked out of place. He stood motionless behind a small white ash tree until he saw movement in the undergrowth. This time he spotted an Indian with a hunting shirt.

His first impulse was to leave the knoll to warn Lieutenant Jellison and the drivers what was ahead. The Lieutenant ordered the wagons to double up and for the drivers to keep their muskets handy. He also called the point man and the one at the rear of the column, instructing all of them to take defensive positions inside the wagons. The column kept moving forward. One Indian had climbed a tree to observe the column. He was too far away for their smooth-bore muskets. Drew asked the lieutenant for permission to fire the first shot.

"You can't shoot that far, Drew, but if you want to give it a try, go ahead," the Lieutenant shook his head.

Drew cocked his carbine and took careful aim, supported himself against the side of a sugar maple tree, and pulled the trigger. A sharp echo swept across the forest. The Indian fell head first from his perch in the tree.

The Lieutenant was impressed. "Great shooting, Drew. Hurry up and reload. We may get a rush if there are many of them."

"Your premonition is correct, Lieutenant. Here they come, about a half dozen of them," Drew yelled, ramming a fresh charge into his carbine. He aimed and fired three times before the band reached the wagons. The attack came to a halt as one of the soldiers stood to eliminate the last brave who had discharged his French musket.

The skirmish was short and deadly. The Indians had shot several times into the wagon train. One driver was slightly injured in the calf of his left leg, but was able to continue driving the wagon. Luckily none of the horses were lost in the exchange of fire. Lieutenant Jellison ordered the wagons forward as rapidly as possible after they had collected the muskets from the dead Indians.

The scows on the river had outrun the wagon train as Drew took his position on the left flank. The balance of the journey to Fort Halifax was without incident. They arrived just as the sun was setting in the west. The column breathed a sigh of relief as they pulled into the safety of the stockade surrounding the fort with blockhouses at every corner.

The fort was built in 1754 under the authority of Massachusetts Governor Shirley when the atrocities were at their peak. It was built on a prominent elevation at the confluence of the Kennebec and the Sebasticook Rivers. Close by was a popular fishing place for native tribes in the area at the Nequamke Falls. Many friendly Indians still used it. Fish were caught in nets or speared and became a staple food for local tribes. Drew noted in the partial light a reinforced redoubt built on a hill behind the fort. The fort was larger than Western and had a larger garrison of soldiers. It was the most heavily armed fort on the Maine frontier.

Drew was exhausted and welcomed the comfort of a straw-filled wooden pallet for a night's sleep in the barracks building. Just before he fell asleep he reflected on the fact that he had taken the lives of a few men that day. It bothered him some, but he had no remorse. It was kill or be killed, and he instinctively protected himself. Having lived all of his life on the frontier, he had built a defensive hatred for the Abenaki, but not for the other native tribes. He was half Delaware Indian by his mother. The older he grew the more his native legacy became evident. His high cheek bones and darker complexion reflected his birthright. Before he closed his eyes, his last thoughts were for his friend, Pru. He shuddered and felt empty when he recalled how it had been in Acadia.

The wilderness fortress was rudely awakened by gunfire at the falls next to the fort. They rang several times through the morning calm, jolting everyone out of a sound sleep. Drew was startled by the noise and for a moment wondered where he was. Soldiers were scrambling for the door with their muskets while Drew pulled on his moccasins and grabbed his carbine placed under the pallet. He asked a soldier what was going on. The man shrugged his shoulders to say that he didn't know.

The shooting only lasted for a few seconds, but it soon collected a crowd at the falls. He met Captain Hanley, commandant of the garrison at Fort Halifax. "What's wrong, Captain?" Drew asked.

The Captain paused a moment in front of Drew. "Some friendly Indians were attacked while they were fishing at the falls. They've been doing that for generations, and we encourage them to continue. Many of the tribes have greeted our presence with charity and friendship. We've got to learn to live together in peace," the Captain said with a firm set to his jaw.

They ran to the falls together. He had ordered men to bring stretchers to the falls. Two people were lying on the ground where the soldiers had placed them. "Make way," the Captain ordered.

Drew grabbed one end of a stretcher as the soldiers gently placed a young girl dressed in doeskin pants and a hunting frock with colorful ornaments on the front. A soldier grabbed the other end of the stretcher and they rushed to the small infirmary inside the fort. Drew saw blood oozing out of a wound in the young woman's side.

He asked the Captain, "Do you have a doctor at the fort?"

Captain Hanley was carrying one end of another stretcher. He replied a little out of breath, "No, we have to send our sick and wounded down river to Western."

Drew helped to place the girl on a bed, seeing that she was very young. The second patient was also a young man. He had been hit in the right foot. Two soldiers with white aprons examined the two wounded Indians. All they could do was to stop the bleeding and clean and dress the wounds before they were sent to Fort Western.

Captain Hanley motioned him to come outside the infirmary. He was outraged at what had taken place. "I'm not sure if this was the work of Abenaki from Odanak or that of white outlaws who see every Indian as fair game. The two injured young people are twin brother and sister. They're a mixture of Penobscot and Mic Mac blood who have been friends to the white men ever since they were babies. They are completely harmless. I've already sent out a patrol to see if they can pick up any sign of the perpetrators. Are you returning to Western soon, Drew?"

"Yes, Sir. That was my intention. What can I do for you?" Drew asked, anxious to help if he could.

"Two of the scows should be returned to Western. We have two other sick soldiers who need doctors. If I sent the four patients down river in two scows, could I ask you to see that they arrive safely at Western?"

It was a heavy responsibility. It made Drew think of Captain Jones. The fact that Captain Hanley thought him capable enough to do the job made him feel good. "Yes, Sir. I'll do my best."

"Thanks, young man," Captain Hanley replied, slapping him on the shoulder. "Your father, formerly a sergeant in the French marines, must be proud of his son."

Drew beamed from the compliment. "I'm proud of my father and my Delaware mother as well, Sir."

Within a few minutes two scows were outfitted with two swivel guns and several layers of blankets and straw for the sick and wounded patients to be placed on. Each scow had a man sitting in the rear with the tiller, a musket at their side and the swivel gun loaded and primed. Drew took his position in the scow closer to the western bank. The two boats entered the river in tandem, giving the smallest profile to any potential enemy on their starboard side. Handling the blunt nose scows through some of the rapids and shallow waters of the upper Kennebec was a tricky business, and the tiller men had their hands full.

Three hours later, Drew could see the British flag flying above Fort Western in the distance. He felt relieved that the sick and wounded could now get the care of a doctor. He relaxed his study of the shore and watched the fort come into view. He saw a soldier and a woman sitting on a rock outside of the stockade fence. He quickly recognized Pru and Corporal Mason, who waved as the scows glided past them. Drew turned away. He felt sick to his stomach!

# Chapter Nine

Drew helped the soldiers carry the two young Penobscots into the Fort Western hospital. The young Indian maiden opened her eyes. They were filled with fear. The look touched Drew who tried to comfort her. "Don't be afraid. You've been hurt, and we're bringing you to get some help. Your brother is here with you. Do you understand?"

She closed her eyes and nodded her head as if she understood. Seconds later, she was being cared for by the British doctor. He saw Captain Howard approaching him.

"You had a busy visit to Fort Halifax, young man. Captain Hanley has written that you handled yourself very commendably. I want to thank you for helping out. Please help yourself to the food at the mess hall. Venison stew and apple pies are a staple here at the fort." Captain Howard motioned to the hall.

"I am hungry, Captain. Thanks for the support. I hope to return shortly. Do you, by chance, have a canoe available?" Drew smiled.

"I don't blame you, Drew. Why don't you go and refresh yourself? I'll see you after I check on a few things."

"You'll know where to find me, Captain Howard," Drew replied.

He helped himself to a large bowl of venison stew and a steaming hot cup of tea before taking a seat facing the warm fireplace. Moments later, Pru came to sit beside him. She was troubled, and it showed in her red eyes. "You're the talk of the fort, Drew."

He modestly shrugged his shoulders. "I did what anyone else would do in my place. We simply brought in two wounded Penobscot Indians."

"I heard that, too," she replied, watching him eat heartily.

"You don't look so good, Pru. What's wrong?" he asked, remembering how she had been traumatized by the untimely death of her mother.

She sighed and focused on the red embers in the fireplace. "I don't know what it is, Drew, but I can't shake off the hurt that my decisions and actions have done to you who doesn't deserve to be hurt..."

"Then why did you do it so quickly, Pru?"

"If I had it to do over again I'd wait a little longer," she quickly confessed. "Seeing the forlorn look in your eyes has touched me and made me feel guilty. I'd like to erase those ugly thoughts that are troubling you. I never thought that my decision while you were at sea would affect you so strongly. The things we said and did as kids are pleasant memories, but they can't be taken as promises for the future. We were just kids, Drew...just kids," she cried helplessly.

Drew hung onto every word she said, remembering how it had been. Had he taken their childish whims too seriously, or had she totally disregarded them as insignificant? Perhaps both had erred on their importance.

He was uncomfortable seeing her so distraught. "Let me say this, Pru. Friendship as adults is not the same as when we were young and impressionable infants. I can honestly tell you that you were my best friend. I was confident, as much as a child can be assured, that I loved you without question..."

"Please, don't go back there..."

"Listen, Pru," he exclaimed. "This has got to be said. I may never get the chance to tell you in the future. Your affection for me was just as well-intentioned as mine for you. That was then. Now we're stepping into adulthood, and things are different as we grow older. You changed, and so have I, even if I did hang on to innocent times a little bit longer. Do not grieve for us. We both have a whole world to explore ahead of us. Place those very special memories of childhood in the back of your mind where you can recall them whenever the time is right. You and

Joseph have my blessings. Don't let fantasies of the past rob you of happiness. I'll be all right. I just need a little more growing-up time, that's all."

She leaned over to kiss him on the lips and whispered, "Oh, my dear friend, Drew." Before he could respond, she ran out the door, leaving him with his thoughts.

Drew stayed on at the fort that night at the request of Captain Howard. That evening, Abel and John arrived at the fort to deliver hay and sawdust to the stables. Later, father and son sat quietly in front of the dimly lit mess hall and talked about the future and where did they go from here? It was an intriguing discussion when Drew saw a rewarding vision for the LeClair family.

The first bit of news Abel shared with his son was his plans to build a ferry across the Kennebec River slightly north above the house where a roadway was already in use since they had purchased the land. There was an increasing amount of traffic on the river as well as on land, connecting parts of the interior with the ocean frontage acres. An inn could be built later. Abel confided to his son that he had assisted in building a ferry when he was a very young soldier in Ohio.

The actual ferry barge or boat should be strong enough to comfortably hold a heavy team of horses and a heavily loaded wagon all at the same time. His father told him that the boatyard could build one very easily. The only other requirements were plenty of long ropes to secure and control the ferry when suitable ramps were constructed on each bank of the river. The ferry could be propelled to either side of the river by the constant flow of fresh water toward the sea with a long rope acting like a pendulum on a clock. One sling of rope would be attached permanently to the east side of the river to sling the ferry to the west bank and the west side of the river to send the ferry to the east. Of course the opposing sling would become shorter and unusable until the ferry was reversed. It acted exactly like a clock's pendulum which swung from side to side in the exact same place every time. It was an old army trick used for centuries to traverse streams.

Drew was excited about the prospect and was anxious to get started. The Inn next to the house would have to wait until the ferry proved profitable. Their dreams anticipated a peaceful resting place for the wilderness travelers. More and more travelers were coming in by ship and many landowners used roadways across the land to sell products and to purchase goods for home and farm.

"You're more of an entrepreneur than I expected, Father," Drew exclaimed. "Are you sure Mother wants to do this? It's a lot of work, and you two are not old, but you are getting older."

Abel laughed at his son. "No one knows that any better than we do, Son, that's why we would like to get it completed this coming winter. We want you to know that you're free to follow your own dreams and wishes, regardless of what they are, son. If by chance you wanted to run the two enterprises, they are yours for the asking."

For the balance of the evening, Drew was quiet and reflective. He was still too young to know what he wanted to do with his life. His introduction to the sea had been a favorable one, but he was unsure of the future. Pru's engagement had thrown him off balance. He saw how his father was so enthusiastic about the future and replied: "I'm going to look forward to making your dreams come true, Father. Maybe in the process, I'll be able to find my own way."

"You're already thinking like a man, son. Let's go to bed. I'm tired."

That next morning, Abel was visiting with Captain Howard in the mess hall when Drew walked into the facility looking for tea and breakfast. Pru was waiting for him to show up. Her color was better this morning. The red eyes had disappeared as well as the heavy lines around her mouth.

"Good morning, Drew," she greeted him. "Would you like some oatmeal?"

"That would taste good, Pru. You look more like yourself this morning. I'm happy for that."

"Thanks, Drew. I needed that talk we had last night. Your father was the first one in here this morning," Pru told him.

"He wants to build a ferry across the river. He's pretty ambitious," Drew smiled at her. "I'm going to help him get it going this winter. We'll see each other around." He accepted his bowl of oatmeal from Pru and went to sit beside his father.

Abel and Captain Howard had just agreed on something, and the Captain left the room in a hurry. "You were sleeping soundly when I got up," Abel said, filling his clay pipe with burley tobacco from Virginia. "The Captain and I just agreed on something that will affect you and your mother. I hope I haven't stepped out of bounds."

"What kind of project, Father?"

"Well, you know what we talked about last night? In order to make those dreams come true, we'll have to hire help in the future."

"Of course, Father. That was logical," Drew agreed. "What did Captain Howard have to do with it? Did you hire him?"

"Oh, no. I agreed to take the Penobscot Indians you brought from Fort Halifax home with us. They are twins about your age, as you know. They have no family. Their parents died from smallpox recently, leaving them on their own. They've attended the Moravian mission in Vermont for the past two years. They learned to speak and write English. My reason for offering them a home was not that charitable. They can contribute as time goes by to our two enterprises. What do you think, Drew?"

"Wow, you make decisions on the spot, don't you?" Drew said, thinking about the potential additions to the family circle. "I have a feeling that mother will approve of your actions. As for me, I have to say that my heart went out to them when I saw how they were viciously attacked without being a threat to anyone. I embrace your kindness, Father. I believe you have given hope for the future to two Native Americans. Do you know what their names are?"

"Yes, the girl is called Amelia and her brother is Ben. Their last name is not known, if it exists. If things work out well, we could adopt them and give them our name."

"I think it's the right thing to do, Father. Now, all you've got to do is find out if Ben and Amelia want the same things."

"Captain Howard is on his way right now to determine that. The doctor is with them this morning. Ben may have a deformed foot from the wound. The Doctor said that Amelia will be fine as soon as her wound heals. She does have a broken rib that will be hurtful for a while, but should heal completely."

His father suddenly became somber and quiet as if he was having second thoughts on the subject. Drew saw the change of expression on his face and asked what was wrong.

"My God, I hope the children don't think we want to take them into our home to use like negro slaves! If they know anything about us, they'll understand that we have no idea to enslave them. I hope the Captain explains that to them."

"I'm sure it was implied you wanted to give them a chance because they're original Americans. We colonists were not the first to be a part of this vast territory," Drew tried to cheer up his father.

Captain Howard poked his head in the door motioning for Abel and Drew to follow him. He seemed pleased with his errand. Drew was still carrying his carbine slung over his shoulder. They entered the fort infirmary filled with the smell of flaxseed oil and witch hazel. The doctor pointed to two patients sitting up in bed.

The Captain turned towards Abel with a smile. "Abel LeClair, I want you to meet Ben and his sister Amelia. I've explained your offer to them. They'll give you their answer. Also, Ben and Amelia, this young man with the rifle is Abel's son, Drew. He helped to bring you safely from Fort Halifax."

Everyone shook hands silently awaiting what the two had to say. Captain Howard quietly left the room. Amelia was the first to speak. "The good Captain has told me and my brother that you will give us a place to live and work. I speak better English than my brother, so I speak for both." She studied the two men before her and continued in a soft voice. "Our first impression was to accept your generous offer to live a normal life. I have some doubts and fear that we might be used like slaves, and I would rather die than be a slave in the same category of property as a pig or a horse. Can you assure me that will not be so? If you cannot dispel our fears then we must refuse."

Her direct response surprised Abel and Drew. This was a person who spoke her mind! "My son and I understand your doubts and fears. Frequently when things sound too good to be true, they are not. My son is a half Delaware and half French, and I love him dearly. My wife is a Delaware Indian who has taught my son to read and speak English and French. I have no desire to make you or your brother captive workers. No man values freedom more than I. What else can I say? The Captain made a request, and I responded. The decision is yours."

Amelia was hurting from her wound, but she managed to evaluate this man before her and her brother as a person they could trust. He had a strong presence and a kind demeanor that was encouraging. She turned to her brother. "What do you think, Ben? This man has offered us an opportunity that is rare on the frontier."

Ben did not hesitate. "I trust your instincts, Sister. I think he's a man we can trust. I already trust his son."

His answer pleased Amelia. "Then it's settled, Mr. LeClair. We'll be pleased to go with you, and we'll work hard."

"I'm sure you will, young lady. Work is a part of life, but there are other things that are also important. I hope you and Ben can share our good times together. We hope this move will be a happy and rewarding one for both of you. You are a person who expresses herself very well. You have my word that our family will treat you with respect and dignity every human being is entitled."

"My father has said it well, Amelia and Ben. Welcome to our little world. I have a feeling that you will enrich our lives. I hope we can have the same influence on you," Drew added. "Now I'm going to see about getting a boat to carry the four of us home."

Drew left to find Captain Howard supervising the unloading of a fishing boat. He pointed to the boat when Drew asked him about transport for the two Penobscot Indians. "You can take this one as soon as we unload it and wash it down," Captain Howard told him.

Pru saw Drew on the dock and approached him. "The rumor throughout the fort is that you and your father are taking Amelia and Ben to your home, giving them jobs and a place to live," she said.

"That's true, Pru. Father is going to build a ferry and will need more help around the farm," Drew said.

"That sounds exciting," she said hesitantly. "Amelia is a very beautiful girl…"

"Yes, I suppose she is, Pru. She was lucky not to have been killed in the attack."

"Is she more beautiful than me?" Pru asked defiantly.

"I'm not going to answer that question," he responded angrily. "You're wrong to ask, being engaged to another man..."

"What if I had second thoughts about being engaged?" she asked in a wavering voice and ran from the dock.

# Chapter Ten

Drew was experiencing emotional turmoil while he and his father sailed the boat from Fort Western to their home. Amelia was resting quietly on several layers of blankets at the bottom of the small craft watching the sky and overtopping tree canopies. The maple, birch, poplar and beech trees were wearing their most colorful bouquet of bright red and soft yellow with shades of orange mixed in. The display signaled the death of summer, warning those in wonder of Nature's handiwork that winter was just around the corner. Those who denied or were unprepared for the ferocity of the months ahead would experience the wrath of Nature. The colorful display around them was a warning that should be enjoyed and also heeded.

Amelia lay so that she could see Ben sitting beside Drew who was seriously handling the tiller. His father sat in the bow of the boat scanning both sides of the river for any sign of trouble. She thought about the decision she and Ben had made to accompany Mr. LeClair and his son, Drew, to their home down river. She was having second thoughts about the drastic change about to take place in their lives. Their very safety and welfare were now in the hands of total strangers. She wondered if they had made a wise decision and was filled with apprehension.

She believed the broad-shouldered Mr. LeCair, who walked with a limp, yet some reservations remained until events would allow her to discard them. She detected kindness and compassion in the father and son who were willing to accept them as equals. It was a good beginning. She had prayed

73

to her God for some sign in making the decision. The age old question, "Where did the two Penobscot youths go from here?" was frequently on her mind. Life had been a constant struggle just to survive. She yearned for the peace of mind and physical safety that the kindly missionary minister had told her would be their reward if they embraced Jesus Christ as their savior and guardian.

The two twins were the last remaining survivors of their small band of Penobscot and Mic-Mac Indians who had lived for generations in the coastal region of Maine. They were intimately familiar with the Penobscot and Kennebec watershed complex and surrounding territories.

"Are you comfortable, Amelia?" Drew asked, seeing her look from side to side.

"Yes. The doctor at the fort told me the wound will heal as long as I properly dress it every day. The broken rib will take a while to mend. It still hurts when I breathe, but I'm not complaining. I was just admiring the beautiful countryside at this time of year. We always called it harvest time when the tribes get ready for winter."

"I've heard my mother call a full moon in the fall a Harvest Moon. You and Ben will like her. Most people do," Drew said, keeping the boat in mid-stream or closer to the east bank. "My father has very good eyes. He can spot things in the woods that most people would not see. When he's on guard we can be assured of a safe journey."

"You and your father have good reputations at both of the forts on the Kennebec," Ben told him in his clipped dialog. He was not as comfortable speaking English as his sister. He was by nature a very quiet young man who was content to let his sister talk for him. In their tribe, women held most of the positions of leadership. His sister Amelia was a powerful advocate for all Native Americans. The injury to Ben's foot would heal, but the doctor told him that he would have a permanent limp and a deformed foot that eventually might limit his ability to walk or run for long distances.

Twice Abel warned them to be alert and to retain full sail. They were traveling rapidly southward with a brisk wind and a receding tide. Abel never explained why, but Drew knew from experience that when he used that tone of voice, he expected Drew to act accordingly. Drew checked the prime of his carbine.

Three hours after leaving Fort Western, they secured the fishing craft to the LeClair landing. Abel was anxious to check on his wife's safety. One of his friends at the boatyard promised to check on her while he was away. He was relieved when he saw Marie rushing towards them. He leaped on the landing and swept her off her feet in a warm embrace. "We have a surprise for you, my dear."

She saw Ben, with a cane, carefully get out of the boat with Drew. "Mom," Drew exclaimed. "This is Ben. He's come to stay with us along with his sister, Amelia. She's lying down in the boat."

Ben graciously clasped Marie's hand and bowed to her. "We share a similar heritage, young man... Ben," she said, studying the ornamentation on his hunting shirt. "You are a Penobscot Abenaki. I'm a Delaware. We also share the sad fact that we are part of a very small tribe that has survived."

Drew jumped back into the boat to lift Amelia and carry her to the landing. "This is Amelia, Mother. I'll follow you into the house. Amelia is suffering from a bad wound that could have taken her life. The trip has exhausted her. Would you make up the cot next to the fireplace for now?" Abel held the door to the house open for them.

That evening, the extended family gathered around the kitchen fireplace and talked about the future. Abel and Drew were proud of the way Marie welcomed the strangers to their family circle. It was evident that Amelia and Ben were impressed with her sincerity and winning smile. She had a way of touching people's hearts, radiating joy and contentment.

Abel laid out his plans for the ferry and for an extension on the house for an inn once the ferry was operating successfully. There had been a lot of talk about a roadway connecting the scattered settlements along the coast. Small streams could readily be forded without difficulty, but the larger rivers like the Kennebec and the Penobscot needed a ferry or a bridge. Abel had scouted the terrain on both sides of the Kennebec and was confident that their location was ideal for the ferry.

Basically for several miles in each direction, the only impediment to a roadway connected by his proposed ferry were trees. These could be cut and removed for firewood, and the larger logs could be taken to the sawmill at the boatyard for lumber.

The family agreed that while Abel and Drew were busy constructing ramps on each side of the river, the boatyard would build the large ferry. Abel still worked there three days a week. On days he was alone, Drew began to cut and clear the extended roadway on their western side of the river as far as their lot extended.

In the meantime, Marie had insisted on time to bring Amelia and Ben up to a satisfactory level of reading and writing English. Since France was no longer a factor on the frontier, she did not insist on French. Every day Marie devoted some time to the twins' education. She found that they were good students who shared her belief that the native people had to learn to survive in the white man's world. That meant being able to communicate ideas and feelings.

A month after the twins joined their family, Marie announced that she wanted to spread some rosemary, an herb of remembrance, on Rosalee's grave before deeper snow came. It was an ancient custom of her people. Drew insisted on accompanying his mother. Amelia had recovered very well from her wounds and wanted to go along, too. Ben stayed at home to keep the fires burning while Abel was at the boatyard.

Winter had arrived in the Maine woods. Frost and light snow covered the ground. Ponds were frozen with two inches of ice. Heavy snows were not far away. Drew checked the flint and priming of his carbine and slung a powder horn over his shoulder. Traditionally, the forests were secure from attack in the dead of winter, but Drew was not taking any chances and remained alert, constantly scanning both sides of the well-worn pathway between the two homes. He set a leisurely pace.

Amelia was recovering well from her wounds. Her rib still hurt when she breathed heavily or moved erratically. Marie had taken to the twins as if they were her own. Drew had expected that of her. Marie had set up a standard time every day for the lessons in English. Drew was included without exception. He reluctantly gave in to his mother's warning that one never has too much education. Amelia and Ben were willing and apt students.

Marie had expanded the reading and writing exercises to include basic arithmetic and geography. She had a close friend in Lavina Cullen, a native Wyandot Indian who was married to the popular owner of a newspaper in Portsmouth, New Hampshire, called the *COASTAL BEACON*. The two corresponded regularly via packet boats sailing the coastal communities. Lavina also sent her teaching aids, books, and paper supplies to encourage Marie to expand her teaching efforts. In the short time they had grown roots on the Kennebec, she had cultivated an interest among the settlers in developing a school. The population along the river was increasing daily with immigrants from Scotland, Ireland and England.

Now that the war was over, energetic colonists began to take an interest in the improvement of their newfound communities. Schools were universally seen as a necessity. Schools and local self-governing bodies followed the pathfinders' original footsteps giving the region a more solid foundation and a feeling of permanence. Trade along the coast was rapidly expanding once the conflict with France was over.

Drew saw the friendly curl of smoke above the trees from John's chimney. They stopped a moment on the trail to rest. Marie was carrying a satchel with a fresh apple pie for John. Amelia leaned against a large red oak tree to catch her breath.

Marie saw her pause and smiled. "Are we setting too fast a pace for you, Amelia?"

"No," she replied bravely. "It feels good to get outdoors and walk. I read in one of the books you recently got from Portsmouth that a person who has broken a rib should exercise even if it does hurt some."

Marie placed an arm around her shoulders and smiled. "The house is close by. John will be pleased with the pie. He has a passion for anything sweet."

Drew continued to be alert to the surroundings. "He's done a lot of cutting on his land. He's got a good pile of logs ready to be pushed into the river to be taken down to the boatyard. Mr.

Boisvert did not look good to me the last time I saw him at the fort."

Marie thought about their old friend and shook her head. "He's been emotionally devastated by the loss of his wife. I do hope we find him in better spirits. Come, we'll catch a chill if we tarry too long."

They arrived at the Boisvert home to find Prudence carrying firewood into the house. She seemed relieved to see them. She was concerned for her father's state of mind. Marie led the way into the house. Drew slung his carbine over his shoulder and grabbed a large armful of firewood to carry into the house.

John sat in a large rocking chair with his feet almost touching the flickering flames Prudence had been stoking. He perked up seeing his visitors come through the door. He rose to embrace Marie who was still holding the satchel.

She released him and stepped back to look closer into his eyes. "John Boisvert, our friend of many years, you've suffered a grievous loss. It's not for me to criticize the depth of your sorrow, but you have to snap out of this depression which is going to destroy you if you're not careful," she scolded him. "Your daughter needs you, and your friends need you. You've always been a source of strength and inspiration to my Abel. He, too, feels your grief."

John nodded his head in agreement. He spotted Amelia standing quietly in front of the fire, holding back from the group. "Is this the young lady Prudence told me about?"

"This is Amelia, John. She and her twin brother, Ben, are staying with us." Marie turned to Amelia. "This gentle man is John Boisvert, Prudence's father and our best friend."

"Welcome to our home, Amelia. The frontier is filled with tragic stories. I've been consumed by my own loss thinking very selfishly that I alone suffer. I understand that you and your brother are also part of our mourning community. Please, remove your coats and warm yourselves by the fire. There's a nip in the air today."

Amelia answered her in a unique soft voice, "Thank you, Mr. Boisvert. We are fortunate to be a part of the LeClair family."

"I brought along an apple pie for your enjoyment. While I'm still dressed, I want to visit Rosalee's grave for a moment," Marie announced.

Amelia buttoned her coat, "May I go with you, Mrs. LeClair?"

"Why, yes, Amelia. We won't be long, John. A hot cup of tea would be nice after."

"Your wish is my command, Marie," John replied, reaching for the teakettle hanging on a hook in the fireplace.

Drew also went to Rosalee's grave with his mother and Amelia. Prudence rushed to put on a heavy coat and scarf around her head, following beside Drew.

The freshly dug grave was coated with a light snow. It was dug on a knoll beside the house with a view of the house and river. The solemn group approached it in silence. Marie stood at the foot of the grave and silently said good-bye to an old friend who had passed on a rich legacy of love and devotion. Marie then kneeled at the foot of the grave, removed a candle from her coat pocket, and placed it on the grave. Drew sprinkled a few grains of gunpowder from a small pistol on the top of the candle, then cocked the pistol, holding a finger over the fire hole. As he pulled the trigger the hammer with the flint sent a spark into the gunpowder on the candle, igniting it.

Marie sprinkled a few sprigs of rosemary all around the grave and candle. "This light is a symbol of our affection for you, Rosalee. May it guide you in your life beyond the sunset. We cherish your memory and pray for your soul and for your mourning husband. Rest in peace, good friend. Rest in peace…" Prudence stood like a statue in front of the grave, oblivious to the cold north winds swirling around them.

Amelia watched the solemn Marie. Tears filled her brown eyes. The scene brought back memories of her parents' death. Loss of loved ones leaves a permanent emptiness that is never overcome. She was touched by the grief wracking Prudence standing mesmerized by her mother's grave. Amelia went up to stand beside Prudence, placing an arm about her waist to comfort her, and whispered in her ear, "I share your loss. Loved ones are always with us in spirit, and death has not diminished their love for us."

Prudence heard the soft voice in her ear and embraced the young Penobscot, weeping on her shoulder.

# Chapter Eleven

Ten Years Later – Spring, 1770

The peace treaty between France and England was finally signed by both parties in 1764. England officially was in complete control of Canada and Colonial America. Most of the colonists had direct ties to the motherland and were proud of their heritage. However, they considered themselves more Americans than English. Parliament was concerned with the expense of carrying on the war against France. The members honestly believed that the colonists should bear some burden in paying the debt to free them of the obnoxious French. Therefore, Parliament began to regulate and tax the colonies in an effort to control the disenfranchised and ungrateful colonists.

The British maintained their arrogant, elitist attitudes toward the settlers, believing them to be unruly and disrespectful to proper authority. The right to own land and to reap the profits of their labor had cultivated an independent streak that defined the colonists to the disgust of Parliament. Revenues were imposed on a multitude of items such as sugar, tea, coffee, porcelain products, paper, etc. For several years a very lucrative trade in smuggling goods had been carried on by adventuresome ship owners throughout the eastern seaboard. They picked up goods in the Caribbean and distributed them to eager purchasers free of duty taxes.

The tax acts were enforced along the coast by heavily armed British schooners and larger gunships of the Royal Navy. The interference of daily trade which had become a way of life to many along the coast, was universally opposed by the colonists. The coastline was filled with small bays and inlets much like the jagged Kennebec and Penobscot coastal mouth. That area in Maine supported a very prosperous shipbuilding industry that flourished as the tax acts increased. Parliament considered most of the ships to be illicit. England rabidly forbid any manufacturing to take place within the colonies. It was expected that anything they needed could be manufactured in England and sold in the colonies. Obviously, many intrepid colonists objected to that monopoly. Distributing the illicit goods was a profitable business until one got caught by one of the revenue packets that diligently patrolled the coast.

The most favored ship for the trade business was a schooner about seventy feet long, with a shallow draft capability in order to navigate close to shore where larger Royal Navy gunships could not travel. Schooners have two masts fore and aft with the main mast being near mid-ship. They could be operated with a crew of six to ten men, and they were relatively cheap to build. The Coburn Shipyard, where Abel had been working until he built his ferry, was briskly building several of the sleek schooners. They had also completed several large merchant ships for foreign business concerns. Shipbuilding was a booming business along the Kennebec and the Penobscot.

Young Drew LeClair was returning home after a two year absence on the schooner owned by Captain Jones from Machias, a small port further north along the coast of Maine. The schooner had been stopped and boarded twice by the Royal Navy, checking to make sure that the manifest and the goods in the hold were legal. If the boarding seamen judged it to be illegal, the goods were either confiscated or thrown overboard. Huge fines accompanied any illegal cargo. The latest had taken place off the Rhode Island coast at Narragansett Bay.

Captain Jones had ordered his small crew not to resist the British sailors when they determined that a portion of their cargo was illegal. When they began to throw overboard kegs of nails and glass, the captain firmly ordered restraint. Risking life and limb for illicit goods was not profitable when the boarding teams outnumbered the crew. Eventually their day of reckoning would come, so they watched in silence, controlling a seething rage that was building all through the maritime community.

Up until two years before, Boston was a popular and profitable port of destination for all kinds of merchandise from the Caribbean, but in 1768 the British had sent two regiments of regulars, under the command of a General Gage, to Boston to police the city and harbor. Resentment by the population was strong, and brawls were commonplace. The seed of discontent was being fertilized by the arrogance of the British occupiers and the complete disconnect of Parliament with the welfare of the colonists. The military occupation of Boston did not diminish the zeal of the privateers. They simply concentrated on those ports like Portsmouth, New Hampshire, Portland, Maine, and Newburyport, Massachusetts, which were more open to trade.

Captain Jones sailed up the Kennebec tying up at the LeClair dock where he unloaded several cases of goods stored in false bottoms overlooked by the nervous British revenue agents. A large cargo net filled with cases of fruits, tea, linens and textile goods from England, and some fine wine from France via Martinique Island were dropped on the LeClair dock.

The most obvious changes to the shore of the river were the increase in numbers of fine houses built since he was last home. The Kennebec community was growing and prospering. There was something magical in returning to his roots. Long voyages far from familiar waters heightened his longing to return. His heart beat a little faster when the ship glided from the rough Atlantic into the calmer waters of the river. The small islands dotting the mouth of the Kennebec were welcome sights. The headwaters of the Kennebec had their source further north at Moosehead Lake. The fresh clear water was soon diluted by salt water from the ocean currents. Drew liked to think that the waters from the large lake were distributed to the far corners of the map, which meant that he was always in friendly waters. It was a childish concept, but it comforted him nevertheless.

The increase in settlers to the region spawned the establishment of churches, schools, and incorporated towns which combated the flourishing lawlessness that accompanied most frontier communities. The river community had its share of thieves and scoundrels who preyed on those most vulnerable. They were controlled by the strict enforcement of law and order. Those settlers who had defended their homes and families against the Abenaki had no trouble in forcing the outlaws to pay a heavy price for their activities.

The schooner delivered mail packets to several of the coastal communities from most every port they visited. Drew had collected newspapers from several ports. They all reflected the growing concern that England had abandoned the welfare of the colonists. Taxes were imposed on almost every kind of activity and were ruthlessly administered.

The LeClair family had built a small inn on the opposite side of the ferry from their original house. The family worked hard to maintain a reputation of excellence. Cleanliness was diligently pursued. They let it be known that families were welcome and that ruffians and drunkards could take their business somewhere else. They had four rooms available for customers in the upper floor of the building. A large fireplace dominated the tavern and dining area on the first floor. It soon became a popular gathering place for the settlers of the area, for travelers up and down the river, and those traveling by roadway with their ferry connecting both sides of the river.

Fresh fish from the river was a daily item on the menu. Kedgeree was a staple food dish the inn served several times a week. It is made from smoked codfish, wild rice collected from the massive beds in Merry Meeting Lake, lentils, beans and hardboiled eggs. Abel and Ben raised several pigs on the property which they butchered. Bacon, hams and other portions of the pigs were cured for several weeks in a special brine Abel developed with sugar, molasses, salt and maple sugar for several months. Then it was smoked in their own smokehouse for several days with green sugar maple wood until it was partially dried on the outside and until the smoke had penetrated through the meat. The smoked items were very popular with the customers. The old smokehouse wreaked with the aroma of the sweetened meats for months after.

Drew was the first to run down the gangplank into the waiting arms of his father. "Our son has returned to us at last,"

Abel exclaimed, embracing him. "How thankful we are to know that you're safe."

Marie had heard Abel's cry of joy and ran to the dock, struggling to hold back the tears of happiness when she saw Drew. He turned from his father's embrace to see his mother flushed with emotion. The first thing he noticed was that she had more white streaks in her black hair. How he loved her gentle ways! He embraced her and gently swung her around in his strong arms.

"We have been so worried for your safety, son. We have much faith in Captain Jones' seamanship, but you have been sailing in a ship the powerful Royal Navy considers an illegal vessel," she cried in between sighs of relief.

"Mother, you worry too much," he said, kissing her on the forehead. "I've felt guilty leaving on such a long voyage with you and Father working so hard to build the ferry and the inn next door. I plan to be more help. I told Captain Jones that this was my last trip out as a privateer. He understood. My urge to see what the world is like beyond our horizons has been satisfied. Home is where I belong. Things have changed on the river. I can't believe the amount of growth that has taken place since I left two years ago."

Abel lifted Drew's heavy duffel bag and followed him and his wife into the kitchen. Drew had six newspapers collected from several printers along the colonial Atlantic coast. It was at Portsmouth that they learned about another tragic incident. A troop of General Gage's soldiers had fired upon a group of unarmed civilians in Boston, killing four and wounding seven. The vicious act was the talk of the town. It soon became known as the "Boston Massacre."

Abel read an account of the incident in the COASTAL BEACON. "Acts of violence like that in Boston add fuel to the fires that are smoldering just below the surface throughout the colonies. Someday it will erupt in such a fashion that it cannot be undone by slick negotiating politicians," Abel predicted with a worried frown. "We're entering a dangerous period. Parliament imposes more and more control on our freedom to act as free men. I fear we cannot win against the most powerful army and navy on earth. Out thirteen separate states have no experience working in unison with each other. United, we could become a potent force, but acting as individual states without any central military command, we're almost powerless."

Drew was surprised with the statement from his father. "Are you suggesting that we should declare war with England, Father?"

Marie placed three hot mugs of tea on the table and sat beside Drew. "That kind of talk frightens me, Abel. Isn't it true that Parliament has repealed several of the duties except for tea? Maybe Parliament realizes that they have gone too far and are willing to be easier on the colonies."

Abel shook his head, smiling at his wife. "My dear lady, your female instincts may be correct, but with the resourceful and independent-minded colonists already outraged with the mother country, something is bound to break the temporary truce — it's a matter of too little too late." Abel stared at the red coals in the fireplace and calmly lit his pipe with a small firebrand.

The conversation around the kitchen table was being repeated all across the thirteen states. Drew listened to his mother and father. He had heard the same arguments at every port the ship had visited. The general atmosphere was explosive. His father was correct. The public was unhappy with the conduct of the mother country. They were still proud to consider themselves Englishmen, and they were true to the roots they had left across the sea. However, they were dissatisfied being treated like errant children. Most of all, the colonists felt that they were capable of taking care of themselves.

That night, Drew retired to his own bedroom and reflected on the solemn conversation with his parents. He had tried to take a more positive position about the situation. Obviously there was much more prosperity building along the coastal communities. His parents were a testament to that fact. He looked out across the landscape to the west where a full moon cast long shadows among the white pine trees silhouetted against the dark mountains in the distance. No longer a child, Drew thought often about the future. He felt secure being home again, but there was something missing... He was always proud of the way his mother and father shared their hopes and dreams with each other. They were never two separate people with individual pursuits, but a couple who faced hardships and joys together. They both maintained their very independent outlook on life, and they often disagreed on issues. Their differences added to the strength of their union.

Drew stared into the night wondering if he was ever going to be lucky enough to share such a compatible and beautiful relationship. He had discovered the presence of females that frequented taverns all along the eastern seaboard and especially in the Caribbean. Coarseness and shallowness offended him in a woman, and he abhorred those who drank like many drunken sailors. He found little beauty in dark rat-infested corners along the waterfronts and was determined that he wanted more out of life.

The still air was suddenly filled with the refrains of whippoorwills calling each other from different locations. It was a familiar sound he had looked forward to as a young boy. The haunting calls came at about the same time every night. It was almost as if they were welcoming him home. A soft breeze flowed through the pine trees with a soothing whirring sound. The world was embraced by the solitude of the night. Drew stretched out on his bed and surrendered to his fatigue.

The next morning, Drew awoke to the sound of voices coming from the ferry beside the house. Many things had changed since he was home. The fees from the ferry were enough to support the family. It also contributed to the success of the tavern and inn. There was a noticeable increase in east-west travel since the ferry was constructed. The inn had developed a widespread reputation for excellence that made it a financial success, thanks to the hard work of Ben and Amelia. Amelia turned out to be a very competent manager. At first, her ethnic heritage made some people reluctant to stay at the inn or to eat at the tavern. Her very gracious and helpful ways eventually won over most of the traveling public.

Ben let Amelia have her way in running the facility. He kept the dining room clean and maintained the massive fireplaces with an endless supply of firewood. Each room upstairs had its own fireplace. During meal time, Ben helped to serve the guests their food and drink. Rum, spruce beer, and wines when they were available were served in the tavern and in the dining room. If Ben found any guest to be unruly, loud, or threatening, he simply called upon Abel to mediate the situation. He usually physically removed those who had been disruptive and had too much to drink. Few ever held it against him but he still continued with the same policy. It was one reason the facility was usually filled with guests every evening.

Two small rooms had been built off the kitchen of the inn for Amelia and Ben. Each week, Abel and Marie relieved them for a couple of days so that they could have time to themselves.

Drew looked out the window to see a team of horses heading west after driving off the ferry. He quickly freshened up with the basin and pitcher of water on his bureau. His mother was in the kitchen baking bread in the fireplace ovens. The aroma made him hungry. His mother embraced him with moist eyes. She was overjoyed to have her flesh and blood at home again. "How nice it is to hold you in my arms, Drew. As you can see, I'm busy baking bread for the inn and for our own consumption. I'd like to fix breakfast for you, but I'm busy with the dough. Why don't you go over to the inn? Amelia and Ben will be thrilled to see you again. She'll be happy to fill you with a hearty breakfast."

"That sounds great, Mother. How have the twins worked out?" he asked with interest.

"They are two remarkable people. They were born and raised in the northern forests of Maine, yet once they were introduced to an education including reading and writing, they embraced the opportunity with a passion few people possess. They are Christians who have displayed more manners and courtesies than many white folk. We are very proud of them and love them as if they were family. You'll find out for yourself, son."

"I remember how eager they both were to receive your lessons," Drew recalled. "I'm glad things worked out for everybody. Father told me that a school has been built down by the boatyard."

"Amelia teaches English one day a week at the school. Several local Indians have attended the school," his mother proudly announced.

"I'm going over for a bite to eat, Mother."

"Enjoy the day, son."

Drew gave his mother a quick kiss on the cheek and briskly stepped out of the house, taking the well-worn path across the new road to the inn. His father waved to him from the east side of the river. Amelia had just finished serving breakfast to a patron and was cleaning up the tables when she saw Drew enter the side door beside the woodshed. She ran to greet him. She was dressed in her traditional doeskin dress under a long white apron. Her hair was done up in two braids that hung down to her waist with two red ribbons tied on the ends She swept across the room in a fluid, gliding motion.

"We knew that you had come home when we saw the ship tie up at the dock," she cried, embracing him. "We've missed you, Drew. My, you've grown since we last saw you. Come, sit at one of the tables. I'll get you a hot tea."

He smiled at her enthusiasm. It pleased him. "You continue to grow lovelier with time, Amelia. It's nice to be home and especially nice to be missed," he replied, releasing her.

She rushed to the kitchen and shortly returned with two cups of hot tea and a steaming bowl of hasty pudding made with ground corn. She smiled when he reached for the bottle of honey, pouring a generous serving onto the hasty pudding.

"Thanks for the breakfast, Amelia. I guess I'm addicted to the sweet stuff like my father."

She took a seat at the table opposite him and relaxed with a cup of tea. "I feel guilty drinking this stuff. The evil herb is tasty. How cruel it is for the Crown to still tax us for its use," she exclaimed with a grin. No tax had been paid for this tea! "Now, can you tell me about your travels? Is the situation as bad as your father suggests?"

He was amused at her interest and replied, "Captain Jones avoids the British ships whenever possible. We never entered ports when there was a strong British presence like Boston Harbor. My evaluation of the general feelings of the colonists is that they are prepared to resist the British. All it will take to unleash the built-up tensions is some event that spills blood. Talk of independence is growing stronger and stronger. I agree with their sentiments, but I don't see how we could possibly fight and defeat the British army. A few years ago the French and their allies could not defeat them. How can we with no standing army or navy expect to do it? I'm concerned that a disaster lurks just around the corner."

"Your assessments reflect your maturity, Drew. I'm concerned too, because I've found happiness and contentment for the first time in my life. Before you carried us down the river from Fort Halifax I was constantly frightened for Ben and myself. At one time, my people freely roamed this land of plenty. Now, all that is left of our tribe can be counted on one hand. War and disease have all but destroyed the proud Penobscot and other small tribes that prospered before the presence of white men."

Drew felt uncomfortable with her strong statement. He was totally aware of the sad decline of the original natives. "Should I interpret that to mean the white men are the cause of their destruction?"

She detected the defensiveness of his question and looked him squarely in the eyes. "The coming of the white man and his Christianity was inevitable. If I sounded angry, please forgive me. I did not mean to blame the white people for our decline. It has been taking place long before you came to our shores. Stronger and more aggressive Indians of our own Abenaki heritage killed and tortured many of the weaker tribes who stood in their way of power and possession of the land. The white men proved to be not much different. Control of the land drives mankind no matter the color of their skin. Outright ownership such as the English believe, is not that much different from the traditional rights concept practiced by the Abenaki," she exclaimed, emotionally answering his question.

Drew took a swallow of tea and a spoonful of corn, contemplating her reply. She turned her head to avoid his scrutiny. She was beautiful by any standard. He reached out to hold her hand across the table. "The first time I saw you at Fort Halifax I said to myself, 'there is a remarkable young lady.' Today I think the same thing, Amelia. Do not forget that I have the blood of my mother and of my father flowing through my veins. I do not stand in judgment of the Native Americans or the white settlers from across the sea. I do not see you as either white or red. I see you as a wonderful person who has won the affection of my family. Did anyone ever tell you that you are very beautiful?"

She looked up to see who had just entered the tavern. Suddenly her eyes filled with fear, like that of a trapped animal, and she quickly ran into the kitchen.

# Chapter Twelve

Drew looked towards the door to see who was responsible for Amelia's sudden departure without a word. He saw a young man about his age with a heavy beard. Drew had a feeling that he should know the man, but could not place him. The stranger looked around the tavern noting that it was empty except for Drew who was sitting at a table eating breakfast. He recognized him and confidently took a seat at the table with him.

"You may not remember me, but I'm Joseph Mason, Prudence's husband. I met you at Fort Western a few years back. I didn't know you had returned."

"Now I recall. You were a soldier at the fort at that time," Drew said. "If you'll excuse me, something unusual took place with Amelia when you entered the tavern. I'm concerned for her."

The outside kitchen door was wide open. Drew rushed through it to find Amelia sitting on a wood chopping block with tears streaming down her face.

"What's wrong, Amelia?" he asked firmly. "Don't tell me it's nothing. I've seen that look of fear and desperation before. Is Mason the source of your fear?"

She stood up to confront him, wiping her eyes dry with a handkerchief. "I warned him to never come back," she cried. "He has tried to force himself on me several times, calling me vile names, savagely demanding that I submit to his desires, or he'll get me fired. What has hurt the most is that he made me feel ashamed of what I am..."

When she was finished, Drew believed her. She was pale white and uncertain what was going to happen. He gently sat her back down on the chopping block. "You rest a few minutes, Amelia. This brute won't bother you again," he promised, returning to the tavern.

Mason was still sitting at the table with a smirk on his face. His arrogant air angered Drew. He could not help wondering what his childhood friend, Pru, would think of her husband if she knew about his obnoxious behavior. "Joseph Mason, you have one minute to vacate the premises. You are no longer welcome at this facility. You've insulted my friend, Amelia, with your foul threats, and you've violated a sacred trust made to your wife who is a long-time friend of mine. Do I hear an apology that any gentleman would be anxious to make, or are you going to simply be an English swine?"

The last characterization infuriated Mason who stood his ground to confront Drew. "You've been misled by the Penobscot. She made me think she liked the attention..."

"What has Prudence to say about Amelia's accusations?" Drew asked angrily.

"That's none of your business, mister-know-it-all. Don't forget, the British still control Canada and the colonies," Mason curtly replied.

"Time's up," said Drew calmly. "You're going to leave this tavern. How you leave is your choice. I hope you resist removal..."

Mason saw the deadly stare in Drew's eyes and bolted for the door, pausing to spit on the floor. "The Indian bitch is not worth fighting about anyway."

Drew was unable to control himself and rushed to propel Mason across the threshold, whirling him around to deliver a hard right to Mason's stomach. "You have the manners and big mouth of a coward. Now get out of here and don't come back."

Mason was slightly doubled over, hanging onto his stomach as he ran along the bank of the river. Drew was breathing heavily, upset with the turn of events. He was concerned for Amelia and his friend, Pru.

Amelia had entered the tavern and approached him. "Thank you for dealing with Mason. I have not confided his actions to either your mother or father."

"Amelia," he protested loudly, you should have done that as soon as it happened!"

"I know that now," she exclaimed. "I was hoping it would pass away. He had been drinking the first time he approached me."

"Promise me that you'll tell me or my father the minute you detect a problem regardless of who the person is. Promise?"

She smiled at him. "I think you handled Mason very well. Your breakfast will get cold." She motioned for him to sit down and took a seat beside him peeling apples. "I have work to do."

"How do you think Pru handles her husband's unfaithful actions?" he asked in a reflective mood.

Amelia saw the worried look on his face. "Your friend, Prudence, is a very unhappy person. Her father has been sickly for a long time and requires much care. Prudence cares for him and her baby girl, Pearl. She also works long hours at the trading post when her father is unable to. Her husband, Mason, helps when shipments arrive at their loading dock and spends a lot of time piloting ships up the river to Fort Western even though it is not an active installation at this time. He acts as if he had no obligation to care for his daughter or his wife. He gambles and drinks a lot. I feel sorry for Prudence who puts on a brave face to cover up his actions."

Drew was surprised to learn how bad things were at the Boisvert household. "How sickly is Mr. Boisvert? Can he still work at the trading post?"

"He does maybe a couple of days each week. Your father helps out some, too. Prudence and I have become good friends. Little Pearl is such a good child. I never had the heart to tell Prudence about her husband. My instincts tell me she knows. Her grief and sorrow are difficult to hide. Her discovery of his ways must be a bitter fact to accept."

"I'm glad she has you for a friend, Amelia. You're a very perceptive person. I'm going to check out a few acres of hardwoods on the property for cutting into firewood." Drew stood up from the table. "Thanks for breakfast. Maybe I'll stop by to visit with Pru and Mr. Boisvert. Should I tell Pru what happened this morning?"

The question made Amelia a little nervous. "If you don't mind, I'd like to explain things to her when the time is right. Who knows? Maybe her husband will change his ways."

"It's nice to be back home. We were lucky when you and Ben became a part of our family."

She smiled again. "Thank you for that, Drew. If you see Pru, tell her I'll stop by this coming weekend."

Drew left the tavern just as his father tied up the ferry to the west bank of the river and hailed his son. "I just saw Mason leaving the tavern. He seemed predisposed. What happened, Drew?"

The situation was serious enough for his father to know just how out of bounds Pru's husband's actions really were, so he told his father everything. "Amelia has been troubled by this for some time, and was reluctant to tell you or Mother. I thought you should know, Father."

"I've known that Mason can be a nuisance and unruly when he has been drinking. I've personally escorted him from the tavern a few times. You handled him correctly, son. Be careful. He's a coward at heart and won't take too kindly to being intimidated in front of Amelia. If it wasn't for John and Pru I would have treated him more severely."

"I'm on my way to the Boisvert's home. Amelia thinks I should not bring up the subject to Pru. She promised to do so the next time she visits the trading post."

"I'm sure an old friend's council will be welcome," Abel said. "I've also been concerned about some measures recently passed by Parliament that probably will be viewed with alarm to some of our more prejudiced colonists. The new Quebec Act has granted freedom of religion to Catholics in Canada and restored French civil law. Poor John, a devout Catholic, may have some reservations about the decisions he has made. This new policy may give him pause about settling here on the Kennebec. Try to convey to him that his friends, and there are many, will always be loyal. Those who view Catholics with prejudice are simply misguided."

95

The act his father mentioned had been the topic of conversation among his shipmates on the schooner. Most, including himself, thought the decision by Parliament was a very logical step in the development of Canada. Human rights were not universally given to subjects by governments.

"Well, Father, you have a customer on the east bank," Drew pointed across the river. "I'll see you when I get back."

"Duty calls. It's nice to have my son home again."

As Drew approached the Boisvert trading post, he noticed how small the pile of firewood was stacked against the south wall. Normally it would be several cords piled in advance so that it could be dried before use. Drew and his father were sticklers for seasoned firewood. John saw him down the path while he was gathering an armful of wood. Drew rushed to his side to help.

"My, my young Drew," John exclaimed, embracing him. "You've grown into a man since I last saw you. How did you like being a sailor?"

Pleased with the warm reception, Drew saw the dark circles under John's eyes and the harsh lines around his mouth. He had lost weight! "I think I'm better suited to work on land rather than the ocean. It's nice to see you, Mr. Boisvert. You have some customers I see."

"Business has increased steadily since I took your father's advice to build the trading post," John remarked, placing his armful of wood beside the fireplace. "If you'll excuse me, Drew. Pru is feeding little Pearl in the house. She'll be happy to see an old friend."

"Is there anything I can do to help you, Mr. Boisvert?"

"Thanks just the same. I'm doing just fine."

John had said nothing about Joseph being in the house. He did not want to confront him with Pru present. She would quickly perceive that something was wrong and start to ask questions. Pru was alone in the kitchen with Pearl when she saw him leave the trading post. She would recognize him anywhere even though he had grown taller and was a little heavier than when she last saw him. There was something wholesome about him that flooded her head with warm memories. She met him at the side door leading into the kitchen with a tremulous voice.

"My dear friend has returned to us. I was worried that something had happened to you." She held him close and laid her head against his chest.

He held her in a strong embrace, softly kissing her forehead. "It's been a while, Pru. I was anxious to see how you're doing. I understand your daughter, Pearl, is the joy of the neighborhood." He was uneasy that Joseph might see them in an embrace and quickly released her. "You're as pretty as ever, Pru."

She looked up at him with tears slowly clouding her vision.

"My husband thinks differently," she cried, pointing to the pock marks on her right cheek from her bout with smallpox. "He thinks they're ugly…" She reached out again to wrap her arms around him and wept softly.

Stunned by Pru's reaction to his presence, Drew looked over her head at Pearl who was frightened by her mother's tears. He felt helpless to comfort her. "Pru, your daughter is alarmed, and I'm concerned for you, too."

"Mommy cry…" Pearl said, climbing down from her chair at the table, rushing to her mother, clasping her arms around her legs.

"I'm sorry… I didn't mean to carry on like this," Pru explained, releasing Drew and kneeling to take Pearl into her arms. "This is my daughter. She's two years old…" Pru turned away from Drew with tears still running down her cheeks.

Silence filled the room as Pru comforted Pearl in her arms. Drew was touched by her emotional outbreak. He remembered what Amelia had told him. "It hurts to see you like this, Pru. Your daughter looks a lot like you when you were small. I can remember those times in Acadia. They sustained me on those long nights standing watch on the schooner. Things have changed, and that's the way life is. If your plans did not work out, you at least have little Pearl."

She looked up at him with sadness. "Yes, I have Pearl, and she is a joy to her mother, but I have little else…!" Her beseeching eyes filled with tears of desperation. Despair consumed her…

# Chapter Thirteen

The intensity of Pru's reaction to his presence concerned him. It was not like her to lose control so quickly. Pearl desperately clung to her mother, frightened by the high pitched scream.

"Pru, for God's sake, pull yourself together!" Drew responded to her outburst. "You're scaring little Pearl and me, too. Surely with such a lovely daughter you have something to be thankful for."

His words calmed her. She reached to comfort Pearl. Her father, John, burst into the room. "I heard the baby crying. What's going on?"

"I'm afraid I started it, Mr. Boisvert. I asked Pru how things were going, and she became very emotional. I apologize for the disturbance," Drew told him.

Normally, John Boisvert would have taken control of the situation, demanding that whatever caused his granddaughter to become upset should end. Instead, he slowly turned to leave without a word. Drew was amazed how out-of-character his conduct was. When he turned his back on Pru, she became infuriated and screamed: "Don't leave, Papa. You know what's wrong. Tell Drew the truth. Please..."

Drew saw a faraway look on John's face as if he was in another world. "Prudence, our problems should remain in the family and not be discussed with neighbors. I apologize for the intrusion, Drew." With those few words, he continued out the door.

The physical and mental decline of John Boisvert, his father's former commanding officer, was a far cry from the gallant soldier his father had portrayed and Drew had witnessed over the years.

Prudence had carefully peeled a piece of apple for Pearl to eat and defiantly turned to Drew. "What my father refused to tell you is that I became pregnant shortly after you left on Captain Jones's ship. For weeks I tried to figure some way of getting rid of the baby..."

"Is Pearl Joseph's child?" Drew asked pointedly.

"Yes, and my father insisted that we get married. Both Joseph and I were opposed to getting married, but father insisted and arranged for the priest to conduct the ceremony. Now you know what a mess you walked into this morning. My sins have made everybody unhappy, especially father. Joseph continues with his free spirit existence while I live a lie taking care of Pearl and my father, who is not well."

Her heartfelt confession gave Drew a better understanding of the situation. He was saddened that such gross unhappiness existed within his childhood friend's family. Unsure of himself in this grotesque discovery, he had an urge to leave as soon as possible. He had no magic solutions to the problems that existed, and he was powerless to alleviate the bitterness that permeated the home.

Pru was quick to read his mind. "I know what you're thinking, Drew. You're disgusted with me and my actions. I don't blame you. I'm more disappointed with myself than you or father can imagine."

"What can I say, Pru? Choices have consequences. Am I disappointed with you? Yes, but that doesn't mean that I condemn you. This is hardly what we had visualized for the future, but that really doesn't matter anymore. The important thing is that you and your husband have an obligation to love and care for little Pearl. She's completely innocent in this sordid affair and probably deserves better than either of you have been giving to her..."

"Oh, Drew," Pru interrupted, grasping Pearl to her breast. "If it wasn't for this precious girl, I would have thrown myself into the river to erase all the heartache I've caused."

"My old friend, Pru, would be a good mother," he said, trying to strike a conciliatory note. "I've got to go now. I want to explore some of my father's forestland for firewood production. Now that I'm back home I want to be useful. By the way, Amelia told me to tell you that she would stop by soon."

"We've become good friends. I'll look forward to her visit. I admire her outlook on life. She tells me things like you do. She means well, but no one can ever know what it's like to live in a house where no one talks to each other..." She paused and looked into his searching eyes. "Are you still my friend, Drew?"

"I never stopped being your friend, Pru. We go back too far for that to ever change."

His words eased the lines around her eyes. She kissed him on the cheek as he stepped out the door. He was anxious to leave. The web of uncertainty and disillusionment had engulfed Pru, and that fact angered him. She was a victim of poor judgment and was suffering for the choice. He was powerless to change that basic fact. For the first time in his life he saw in Pru a streak of self-pity that worried him the most.

Drew had a desire to be alone and picked up an old trail that he and his father had first established to get at the hardwood stands to the western backland. Firewood production was a necessary fact of life on the frontier. The LeClair family used over twenty-five cords of well-seasoned firewood each year. That translated to over two cords per month that had to be produced just to maintain a steady supply.

The need for firewood whetted Abel's desire for additional land. When two additional forty acre tracts became available, he quickly purchased them, giving them a total of one hundred and twenty acres. Most of the land was covered with white pine, hemlock and assorted species of hardwood such as oaks, maples, birches and beech. Abel and Drew had cut some of the larger trees for logs and sold them to the sawmill at the boatyard. The forest resource was a valuable asset which his father managed with an eye for the future. Careful management would supply the tavern and home with all of their firewood needs forever. Balancing yield and harvest with growth was a reflection of the husbandry Abel applied to the land. He never allowed the annual harvest of logs and firewood to be greater than the annual growth in the total land tract.

With that example of prudent stewardship on his mind, Drew mentally laid out several acres of red maple, yellow birch, and mixed hardwoods in a small swamp area that could be harvested come winter when they could travel on the ice. There was an improved woods trail that led to the roadway which connected to their ferry. They had enough wood for two years. The drier the firewood, the more heat produced. Therefore, Abel insisted on seasoning the wood for two years. Once that surplus was harvested, all they had to do was to maintain the annual harvest, rotating it every two years.

The harvesting operation required that trees had to be cut into two or three foot lengths to fit the different size fireplaces. Axes and wedges were used to split the larger pieces into smaller sizes for easier handling. Larger logs were difficult to split with wedges, so Drew drilled a small hole into the center of the log several inches deep. Then he filled the cavity with gunpowder and plugged the opening, leaving a short fuse of about ten inches long. He lit the fuse and quickly stepped back from the log. The explosion of the powder split the larger piece of hardwood into smaller, more manageable sections. The operation required steady nerves and an agile foot. Working with wood split with gunpowder gave Drew a headache after an hour or so.

Several hours later, Drew headed eastward toward the river, following a heavily used trail that led up over a granite outcrop overlooking the meadow where they annually cut hay for the animals. The sun was beginning to set behind the mountains to the west, creating small shadows across the landscape. The house and tavern could be seen from the vantage point. Drew and his father had shot several deer and moose from the promontory perch. It was a favorite location for reflection and solitude. Drew stepped out of the shadow of the large white pine trees that dominated the site, surprised to find Amelia sitting beneath one of the trees. He was reluctant to intrude on her privacy.

She spoke first. "I heard you coming, Drew. Your father insisted that I take the rest of the day off from work. I wrapped up a small lunch of apple pies and cheese and came up here to be alone."

"I apologize for interrupting, Amelia."

"You're not interrupting, Drew. Would you like one of my apple pies? The cheddar cheese is fresh from England."

He took a seat next to her against the white pine tree, accepting the offering. "I am hungry. I haven't eaten since this morning. Thank you. Did you get over to see Prudence?"

"Yes, she was still upset," Amelia replied with a long sigh. "I was unable to console her. Today was the first time I've seen her so despondent. We exchanged a few sharp words, and I left so that she could think things over. I came up here to do the same thing."

She watched the glistening of the setting sun on the dark waters of the river. The evening tones and colors changed the appearance of familiar objects. Drew turned to see her better in the fading light. There was a pensive air about her that reflected the depth of her perception which was far greater than his own. He always felt that she was reading more into his words and thoughts than he was able to decipher with her.

She asked him a question that shocked him. "Have you ever wished to be all white instead of part Indian?"

"I don't know how to answer that, Amelia. I've experienced some incidents about my race that angered me, but long ago my mother and father prepared me to ignore those who try to make me feel inferior. No, I've never consciously wanted to be anything but who I am. My father always said we have to play the cards we're dealt. It may be unfair, but that's the way it is. Are you having thoughts like that, Amelia?"

"Sometimes I wonder what it would be like to be a free white woman like Prudence. I understand what you are saying. It is not rational to wish or to contemplate for what can never be… I'm sorry to bring up the subject. I have something to share with you."

Relieved that she was changing the heavy subject, Drew asked, "What is that?"

"Well, several days ago, I received by post a letter from a dear friend in Canada. She's a native Delaware like your mother and just gave birth to a baby girl. We were both at the Moravian mission school for several years. I've missed her friendship. I was afraid she had perished with smallpox or some other disease. Happily, her letter tells me otherwise."

"So she beat the deadly disease like Prudence," he remarked. "She was fortunate. Most people cannot cope with the extreme temperatures."

"I was wondering if your parents would object to my absence if I went to Canada for a short visit to see her before cold weather sets in for good."

"Do you mean by yourself? And how would you go?" Drew asked.

"I've been thinking that I might be able to take a passage on the next merchant ship that made deliveries to the tavern. I could go to Nova Scotia and then up the St. Lawrence River to the outlet of the Chaudiere River near Quebec. I've traveled up the Kennebec several times to the Dead River and then to the Chaudiere. It has been a heavily traveled route for all of the tribes in the region."

"But you could not do it alone, Amelia."

"Ben and I have made the journey several times when we were younger," she replied.

"How long will it take you? Quebec is a long ways from here and we are separated by miles of wilderness. Ben could not make such a trip with his bad foot," he told her, thinking of all the hazards of traveling alone.

Amelia smiled at his concern. "You may not believe it, but I shared my thoughts with Prudence several days ago. She told her husband, Joseph. He showed up at the tavern, a day later, with the news that he had traveled all of the Kennebec several times and that he would escort me to Canada. I outright refused his offer. That was when he started to be abusive and insulting," she confided with a sober expression. "Maybe I could locate one of the Penobscots near Moosehead Lake to accompany me. Actually all of this talk is for nothing if your mother and father do not agree with my leaving. Everybody has been so busy lately."

Drew thought about the voyage, admiring the courage she had for such a visit so far away. He had known Amelia ever since he brought her and Ben to the house from Fort Halifax a few years ago. She was a dedicated employee who displayed an intelligent and artistic flair in everything she did. Always cheerful and open to suggestions, she worked tirelessly for the LeClair family. Yet, after all that time, he still did not know much about her hopes and dreams for the future. She was by choice a loner who functioned gracefully with others, still maintaining that illusive air which defined her as a Native American. He often thought that she was lonely at times even if she would never admit it. The fact that she asked for some time from work was significant, because she rarely asked for anything for herself. She was a giver, not a taker, and Drew and his family admired her generosity.

"I can't speak for my parents, Amelia, but I'm sure they will agree with your request. You've earned some time for yourself. I'll speak to them tonight. Do you want me to do that?"

"I'll appreciate it, Drew. It will be better to make the trip this fall when there are no black flies or mosquitoes to bother. The trip would take about a week travel time one way. My friend Laura will be surprised. We were such good friends."

The sun had completely dropped from sight behind the mountains. Drew helped her stand. "We should be getting back. I've never been past Fort Halifax on the Kennebec. Father has often spoken about Quebec and life in Canada before the British gained control of the region." He looked into her eyes and continued, "I would not feel right having you go alone. Would you mind if I go with you?"

She smiled and grasped his hand. "I never forgot the kindness you showed to me and Ben that day, long ago, when you sailed with us down the river. If I said 'yes' would it be selfish of me to take you away from your family after your long absence?"

"Then your answer is 'yes'?" he grinned.

"My answer is 'yes' provided your parents don't mind."

Later that night, Drew presented Amelia's request to his mother and father. They instantly agreed to her proposal. They would make do by hiring temporary help which was plentiful in the area. He informed Amelia of their approval the next morning and told her they should start to make preparations for the trip. He began by checking on the availability of a lightweight canoe or boat rugged enough for two people and their baggage to tackle the rapids and portages ahead of them.

The traditional birch bark canoe was a very fragile craft that needed frequent repairs. Drew had already made up his mind that he wanted something different. The owner of the boatyard sent him to a local builder of small boats and canoes downriver a few miles. It was an elderly gentleman who specialized in making lightweight canoes made from animal hides stretched and attached to a white ash framework with nails. The craft was then painted with several coats of shellac or varnish which not only stiffened and strengthened the hides, but made them slippery and waterproof at the same time. The hide canoe was about the same weight as a bark canoe. He was impressed and ordered one to take back upriver with him. He attached the canoe to the sailboat and triumphantly sailed back home, pleased with his purchase.

# Chapter Fourteen

Two days after Drew and Amelia decided to make the trip north to Canada, they had accumulated enough food to last for the journey. Their baggage included a small silk tent for Amelia's use at night, and personal items for each of them. Altogether, the cargo weighed about a hundred and fifty pounds, making it light enough for them to drag the canoe and contents around the many portages that confronted them.

They began their journey the first of September, early in the morning while the mist slowly rose from the dark blue water of the Kennebec. Their destination for the first day was the massive falls at Skowhegan. Food and baggage were carefully secured to the canoe so that it would not be dislodged even if they had an upset. Their food supply for the trip included pemmican made of corn, wild rice, blueberries, and dried venison all combined with a generous amount of tallow. It was a tasty and nutritious source of food that remained edible for a long time. Amelia had also included a supply of dried moose and venison meat cut into thin strips, a block of cheddar cheese, a small jar of honey, and tea. She also brought along two loaves of fresh baked barley bread which they planned to eat before it became stale.

The frontier was free of the fierce elements that existed during the war between France and England. However, the vast unsettled wilderness between the Saint Lawrence River in Canada and the coastal regions of Maine was still populated with a certain number of bandits and unsavory characters that preyed on unsuspecting travelers. To counter that threat, Drew was armed with his rifled carbine and a pistol tucked into his belt. He supplied Amelia with another pistol for her to keep on her person. They did not intend to be helpless victims to the few scoundrels that existed.

Amelia rode in the front of the canoe with Drew in the rear. They had timed their departure to coincide with the incoming tide which would make the first few miles on the river much easier to negotiate. Their first portage was at Taconic Falls located a short distance past the remnants of Fort Halifax, which was no longer maintained by the militia. Amelia suggested that they include a coil of rope to their baggage to help drag the canoe around such obstacles, or lift the canoe up over the falls at Skowhegan.

The Skowhegan Falls was a well-known camping site for the native people. Drew was doubtful that they could make it by nightfall. It was forty miles from Fort Western. Amelia had assured him that traveling up the Kennebec to the falls would be the easiest portion of their journey. The long and arduous portages between the Kennebec River and the slow moving Dead River further to the north would be the most difficult. Drew had suggested that they use horses and stick to the trails through the forests, but Amelia was not comfortable riding horseback.

At the end of their first day, the wilderness travelers had exceeded their expectations, arriving at the Skowhegan Falls just as the sun dropped behind the rugged mountain chains to the west. They quickly pulled the canoe up over the falls and began to scour the forest for enough firewood to last the evening. Soon a friendly fire was cracking in a stone enclosure near the northern edge of the flat, forested island in the middle of the river.

The view up the river was filled with orange rays from the disappearing sun. It was a scene that eased their aching muscles. The chain of mountains to the west loomed above them in a semi-circle looking down on their small campsite. They formed a massive granite barrier that extended inland from the Georgia coast all the way to Canada. Its majestic grandeur was highlighted by the final rays of the setting sun — sentinels of the wilderness.

Drew rushed to set up the small silk tent for Amelia while she heated water for tea over the fire. The warmth felt good as the sun disappeared. September in the northern latitudes could be chilly. The fire cooked their food, warmed their bodies, and soothed their souls, cultivating a feeling of good will. A fire soon became the wilderness traveler's best friend.

"Are you as hungry as I am, Amelia?" he asked, searing several thin slices of dried venison over the flames. "We've done well to get this far in one day. I hate to admit it, but your desire to reach this location has worn me out. I couldn't paddle another stroke."

She smiled at him and carefully poured the boiling tea into two tin cups, passing one to him. "I am weary, too, Drew, but this place is worth the effort. September is my favorite time of the year. No black flies or mosquitoes makes life easier. I'll sleep well tonight. The roar of the falls is a soothing sound."

He slowly sipped the steaming tea, watching her stare into the reaching flames. Peace and contentment radiated from her. She had that same positive outlook on life and things around her that he had always admired in his mother. It was a softness that came from living in harmony with whatever environment they happen to be experiencing.

"I'm glad I came along with you, Amelia. I've never been north of the old Fort Halifax ruins. I've heard people describe the falls here the way you have. Now I know why. It's a beautiful spot. If only the rest of the colonies could project the same feeling of well-being... At some point, the discord is going to erupt, and there will be bloodshed over the differences that exist between the colonists and Parliament. My father doesn't believe we can win a war against England, if it comes to that."

"Do you think that it will go that far?" she asked seriously. "I hear talk at the tavern about issues on both sides, and the anger is getting louder and louder. If there is war, what will you do, Drew?"

"My father and I have discussed that possibility. I would definitely want to defend the way of life that we have established here on the Kennebec. I'm not sure, Amelia. Maybe I'd join with Captain Jones and serve on one of his privateers at sea."

She acknowledged his comments with a frown. "The potential for disaster is something I do not want to contemplate. Let's not think about what might be and concentrate on the journey ahead of us. I've been hoping to make it for a long time. I don't want to spoil it by thinking dark thoughts of what may happen in the future."

"You're a realist, Amelia," he grinned, passing her some of the warmed venison strips and some toasted bread with honey.

They ate heartily that evening and were anxious to retire for the night to rest aching limbs. Drew placed his blankets and bearskin in the canoe next to Amelia's silk tent. His last act before closing his eyes was to locate the North Star. His father had told him that it was the only star in the galaxy that did not move. It has been a faithful guide to mankind through the ages. Once the star was located, everything around them could be properly oriented.

"Goodnight, Drew," Amelia called from her tent.

"Rest well, Amelia. As you know, there is nothing in the Maine wilderness that can harm us. The North Star is bright over Quebec. Locating it early in the evening is like finding a faithful friend. I have my pistol and rifle with me under the robe and am a light sleeper, so don't worry about intruders."

"This is not the first time I've placed my life in your hands, Drew. You are truly your father's son. I have no fear."

Her words pleased him. It was a tribute to father and son that touched him.

Hours later, after the fire had been reduced to smoldering ashes, two figures left the dark stand of trees and crept silently to the campsite where they paused to study the scene and make sure they had not been detected. There was a partial moon that evening, giving enough light for the intruders to observe the canoe and the tent. They had watched Amelia from their hidden camp while she refreshed herself at the water's edge before retiring to the tent. The presence of a young Indian maiden whetted their appetite for companionship. They patiently waited several hours before they boldly invaded the sleeping traveler's campsite. Unbeknown to the two men, Drew had heard them and grasped his pistol from under his bear robe.

Without warning, Drew received a heavy blow from a stick across his stomach, momentarily knocking the wind out of him. One man had attacked Drew while the other quietly opened the tent flap and crawled on top of Amelia grasping his hand over her mouth to keep her from screaming.

Drew involuntarily cried out in pain, but his instincts remained true. He grabbed the arm of the attacker forcing him to release the stick and placed the pistol against his body. A flash from the pan ignited the heavy charge of powder in the pistol. The intruder was knocked to the ground. The sound echoed through the wilderness blocking out the muffled screams from Amelia who was frantically fighting her assailant. She kicked and punched the man on top of her and bit his hand. He responded calling her a foul name, releasing his grip over her mouth and slapping her hard across the face.

The sudden impact of her attacker's blow and her loud scream, frightened Drew that Amelia was hurt. He sprang from the canoe throwing the wounded man to one side. Still weakened from the blow he had received, Drew ripped the tent moorings free and grabbed the attacker by the hair, pulling him from Amelia and at the same time delivering a powerful blow to the man's face.

Amelia had pulled herself free of the tent, frightened at what was taking place. She saw Drew repeatedly strike the man in the head and face while holding him in a vice-like grip with his left arm. "Stop it, Drew. He's not worth killing..." she screamed several times.

Drew heard her desperate cry and released his grip just as he drove his knee into the man's groin. The attacker let out a howl of pain and Drew repeated the act dropping the man to the ground. His howls filled the still night air. Drew turned to Amelia and grasped her in his arms; "My God. I'm so sorry for this, Amelia. I should have been more alert to their presence. Did he hurt you?"

"The pig struck me in the face, but I'm okay, Drew. I was so frightened that they had shot you."

"No, I managed to stop him with the pistol. I had no alternative," he answered, shaken by the experience. "Come, let's rekindle the fire so that we can see just who these brutes are."

By the time Drew dragged the wounded man to the side of the fire, propping him against a rock, Amelia had a fire burning brightly with several pieces of white birch bark and some white pine twigs. The man was still conscious, holding his bleeding arm. Drew stripped away his shirt sleeve to check the wound. Amelia wiped away the excess blood and cleaned his arm with a damp cloth. The heavy slug of lead from Drew's pistol had shattered the lower portion of the man's arm.

"There's not much we can do to help you," Drew declared. "What's your name, and where are you from?"

The injured attacker remained silent and defiant. His partner was lying on the ground still whimpering over the treatment he had received from Drew. Amelia cut a section of their rope to tie the man's hands behind his back. He sneered at her. His attitude angered her, and she vigorously kicked him again in the groin. "That's for me, pig. Whine some more."

"Where's your camp?" Drew demanded of the wounded man. "Are you going upriver or downriver?"

He pointed to the east, indicating a heavy stand of young white pine. "Camp is in the woods." Then he pointed downriver.

Drew placed more firewood on the fire and loaded his pistol, motioning for Amelia to follow him out of hearing range of the two men. "What are we going to do with them, Amelia?"

She turned to look back at the two men warming themselves by the fire. "We could let them go. I'm not going to let two brutes spoil this trip to an old friend. We could make them walk if we destroy their canoe or boat."

"I agree with you. First thing in the morning we'll send them on their way. You try to get some sleep. I'll watch our prisoners. Neither of them look very formidable right now."

Later that morning, Drew followed the two men to their campsite. They had a canoe and some provisions. He found two fowling pieces and smashed them against a rock, bending the barrels and breaking the stocks. Drew ordered them to break camp and head downriver. He would be watching them with his rifled carbine, and he would kill them both if they made a false move. He also warned them that if he ever saw them around the Kennebec he would not hesitate to carry out his threat. Ten minutes later, he saw them disappear around a curve in the river and rushed to see if Amelia was still sleeping.

She was looking for his return with a strained look on her face. He told her they had gone downriver. She passed him a hot cup of tea. "We should pack up to leave as soon as possible, Amelia. I hope we didn't make a mistake letting them go."

She looked at him with her sad brown eyes. "Those pigs have darkened my memories of this beautiful place."

He saw that she was anxious to leave. "I understand, Amelia," Drew replied, placing a comforting arm around her. "I'm sorry I could not protect you better."

She rested her head against his chest for several moments. "Do not dwell on what happened," she whispered and kissed him softly on the lips.

# Chapter Fifteen

The trip north to Amelia's friend at Sartigan was completed on the eighth day of travel. It had been a grueling test of their endurance once they had left the Kennebec River traveling over several miles of swampy land to the Dead River, a slow moving body of water running north into Chaudiere Pond. Their course across the lake was a pleasant respite from the shallow swamps filled with dead trees and limbs. After leaving the Pond, they arrived two days later at the small Indian community near Sartigan, several miles south of Quebec.

The arduous journey had brought them to a small log cabin on the east side of the Chaudiere River where Amelia excitedly pointed to a landing dock. Drew directed the canoe to the dock and jumped out to help Amelia. She was all smiles.

It was late in the afternoon. "No one has seen us yet," Drew exclaimed, scanning the level plains around the cabin.

"Laura's going to be surprised," Amelia announced with flushed cheeks. "Leave our stuff in the canoe for now, Drew. We can get it later."

He followed her along a well-worn path leading to the cabin. Suddenly the door opened, and an elderly Indian lady anxiously began speaking in her native tongue. Drew saw her arresting dark eyes stare at them with arms flailing and tears flowing down her bronze face. She was overcome with despair.

Amelia rushed closer to the door, speaking to the lady all the time. The two conversed several seconds in high pitched tones. The elderly lady motioned for Amelia not to come any closer. Amelia stood still and gestured with her hands.

Drew was concerned and impatiently asked, "Amelia, what's wrong?"

Amelia held out her hand to Drew, listening to the elderly lady. Then she turned to him and said in a wavering voice: "This woman has been caring for the family. Laura and her husband died from smallpox a few days ago. Their child is now down with the heavy fever, and they do not expect her to survive..."

Amelia was too choked with emotion to cry. The trip north that had generated so much enthusiasm and anticipation of renewing old friendships had now deteriorated to a tragic ending.

Drew placed an arm around Amelia's shoulder while the elderly Indian woman pointed to a small grove of tall spruce trees close to the landing next to the river. Laura and her husband were buried there. Drew helped to support Amelia and directed her towards the newly dug graves. Two small crosses were lying on top of the red soil. Amelia dropped to her knees and wept uncontrollably for the loss of her best friend. Cries of grief that started in the inner depths of her soul found release piercing her quivering lips at a high crescendo that worried Drew. Large tears grew in her dark eyes, freely dropping on the freshly dug earth. Convulsive sobs echoed across the wilderness.

She wrenched herself free of his grasp onto the grave, continuing her heartfelt sobs. It was a catharsis such as Drew had never witnessed, and he felt helpless to comfort her. For what seemed an eternity, she remained rigidly motionless on the graves. Then she slowly stood up, wiping the tears from her eyes with a linen cloth. She looked across the opening to the small cabin with a plume of gray smoke rising from the chimney, then once again back at the graves.

"Goodbye, dear friend. I'll never forget you. You'll never know how alone your sad passing has made me feel..." Amelia stared at the fresh earth and softly whispered, "Until we meet again, Laura..."

Drew reached out to embrace her. "You're not alone, Amelia... not anymore."

She gently released herself from his embrace, grasping his hand. "Come, Drew, let's go home..."

He helped her down to the small dock and into her position at the front of the canoe. Her dark eyes stared off into the wilderness as if she was searching for something. Drew secured their meager supplies and shook his head. They did not have enough food to make the return trip. He did not mention it to Amelia, but he intended to stop at Chaudiere Pond where he could fish and hunt for moose and venison without leaving Amelia alone. He estimated they could make it to the Pond the second day after they left Sartigan.

That first evening they made camp on the west side of the river in a large white pine grove. He pulled the canoe out of the water with Amelia still sitting silently. He collected enough firewood to last for the night and placed a baited fish line onto a small white ash tree hanging out over the water. There was enough dried codfish and cheese left over from their supply for the next two days. After that they would have to supplement their food supply.

That night, Amelia accepted the fish, cheese, and hot tea Drew served her as she sat against a pine tree next to her tent in front of the fire. After they had eaten he cleaned their plates and cups in the river and prepared her bed in the tent. She sat quietly staring at the flames reaching high into the evening sky. She had not said a word since leaving the graves. He did his best to respect her grief and refrained from idle chatter.

"Your bed is ready for you, Amelia," he said in a low voice. "Is there anything I can do to help?"

Tears welled into her eyes, and she replied in a soft, shaky voice: "You've been wonderful on this trip. Thank you for your kindness. I'm exhausted, and a night's sleep will feel good."

He held out a hand to help her up from the ground. She accepted his assistance and stubbed her foot on a root and fell into his arms. He looked into her dark eyes and gently kissed her on the mouth. It was a normal reaction to the feelings he had cultivated some time ago that had blossomed during this trip. She returned his embrace and rested her head against his chest. It was a moment of discovery for both of them. He held

115

her close to his heart and thanked God for the revelations her kiss represented.

She was first to speak. "I'm overwhelmed, Drew. I was afraid these feelings I've experienced for a long time would not be reciprocated. Tell me that this is real for you, too."

"I think I've loved you ever since I saw you lying helplessly in the boat from Fort Western. This trip has confirmed those impressions. I've fallen in love with you, Amelia. It was easy, you know."

She gently kissed him again and sighed. Overhead she saw a flight of geese in a V formation on their way south for the winter. She interpreted it as a sign of recognition of their love for each other. It confirmed and approved what two young hearts had just discovered.

Their return trip was filled with hardships normal to the route they had chosen, but the joy of doing it together became a treasured memory they would always recall with smiles. They had been lucky at the pond. The first day of their stay, Drew saw a small doe drinking at the water's edge within easy range of his rifled carbine. The animal provided them with adequate food for the rest of the trip.

They were returning as two different people from the ones that embarked upon the journey. Still saddened by her friend's death, Amelia was also buoyed by the love that she had held in her heart, afraid it would never be. Drew dispelled that fear with his gentle and kind ways. They found it easy to convey their inner thoughts to each other. It was a normal transition from the solid friendship they had enjoyed from the very beginning. There was much to love about the soft-spoken Penobscot maiden who gave of herself and asked for nothing in return.

They were both glad to tie up to the LeClair landing. She watched him secure the canoe to the dock. "This is one trip I'll never forget. I lost a dear friend, but at the same time, I discovered something I'll always be thankful for. How nice it is to love and be loved in return."

"I'm a lucky man to have won your love, Amelia. I can't wait to share the good news with Mother and Father," he exclaimed, lifting her out of the canoe.

That fall the LeClair family and close friends were excited about the wedding they were planning. Abel and Marie were not surprised at what had happened to the happy couple. They had seen it coming. Once the two were married, Abel and Marie announced that the couple should take over the tavern and inn and run it as their own. Abel was happy to continue with the ferry, which was more and more profitable as more settlers came to the region. They were almost fifty years old and were looking forward to that day when they might be grandparents. The wedding was scheduled for late in October when the foliage was in full bloom. The bride and groom insisted on a simple affair with a few close friends in attendance.

The day of the wedding, friends and acquaintances flocked to the tavern. Reverend Post, a beloved Moravian minister who had known Amelia when she attended school at the mission in Memphramagog in the New Hampshire Grants, had agreed to perform the wedding. The event turned out to be larger than anticipated, but there was adequate food and drink to properly celebrate the simple country wedding. As expected, Pru came with her father, John, to join in the festivities. Pru sincerely embraced Amelia and Drew and congratulated them. Amelia was dressed in a white gown with a white veil Marie had made for her. She was beautiful. Her white gown highlighted her bronze complexion. Drew was so proud of her. She was the envy of every young lady in the area.

After the ceremony, several local musicians began playing music to dance. They started off with several slow foxtrots and waltz tunes. John and Abel were looking forward to a turn with the new bride while Drew danced with his mother. Marie noticed that Pru was sitting by herself. "Why don't you dance with Pru?" Marie whispered in Drew's ear.

Drew maneuvered toward Pru. "I will, Ma. You look lovely tonight."

"Your father and I are so pleased for you and Amelia."

Pru watched as Drew and his mother approached her. "May I have this dance, Pru?"

Pru smiled and stepped into his waiting arms. "Amelia is a wonderful person. I wish both of you much happiness, Drew."

He replied gracefully, "Thanks, Pru. Today would not be complete without best wishes from an old friend."

Pru's eyes were moist. "Tonight, I lost the only friend I ever had... How differently things turned out!"

"I'll still remain your friend, Pru. It's important for Amelia and me to have your blessing."

"I'm being too sentimental tonight. You and Amelia deserve each other. Of course I bless your union. I keep praying for Joseph to change. I think he's trying, but..."

"I'm sorry, Pru," Drew said, looking into her sad eyes. "You deserved better."

The exchange pleased her. "Your new bride has just finished dancing with your father. Go to her, old friend."

After the festivities, Drew, Amelia and Ben settled down to manage the tavern and inn. As the months rolled by, they had increased its reputation for excellence. The additional patronage reflected the rise in population along the Kennebec River. Ships stopped by regularly to discharge supplies, passengers and news from the lower colonies.

There was a growing insurgency opposing imperial authority and a deep sense of betrayal by the mother country. More and more discontent grew within the citizenry who experienced Parliament controlling more of their lives and taxing them for everything manufactured in England. The taxes on glass, paper and some clothing goods was repealed in 1770, but the tax on tea remained in place. Consequently, the colonists rebelled in the most obvious way possible — they refused to drink tea. Drew and Amelia substituted coffee instead of tea at the inn.

Earlier that same year Amelia and Drew were married, British troops in Boston had fired their muskets into an unruly crowd killing five citizens. The act was an important symptom of the depth of rage and opposition throughout the colonies. One year after their marriage, Amelia gave birth to a baby boy they named Abel, Jr., after Drew's father. It was an important milestone in their union. Little Abel soon dominated every aspect of family activity in the LeClair home.

The joy and happiness which permeated family life after Abel, Jr., was born was altered by the family's concern for

Amelia's health. She had quickly regained strength after giving birth and was soon handling details of management as efficiently as ever. She was displaying her usual capacity for work when she suddenly became very ill and was confined to her bed. There had been an outbreak of smallpox in the area, and it soon became evident that Amelia had contracted the dread disease.

Drew was constantly at her side fighting the high fevers with frequent bathing with cool spring water. The fever wracked Amelia's body, sending her into massive convulsions. She fought the ugly disease with every ounce of energy she possessed, but she was slowly losing the battle.

She remained unconscious for several days until one night when Drew, ravished with dread and pain, was at her side holding her feverish hand in his. She squeezed his hand lightly and then went limp — her God had taken Amelia home. Her quiet passing sent Drew to the fringe of madness with grief and despair. Family and friends were worried about him. Even little Abel could not ease his pain. He was paralyzed with it. Screams of anger and impotence pierced his lips as he clung to the dead body of his precious Amelia. All they shared now were memories of happier days.

# Chapter Sixteen

Four years later, December, 1774

Drew had taken passage on Captain Jones' schooner heading south, planning to get off at Portsmouth, New Hampshire, to purchase supplies for the tavern and inn. He had occasionally met the irascible sailor when he delivered goods from the Caribbean to the tavern. They often talked of the time he sailed with them a few years ago.

There was much excitement and anxiety aboard. The Continental Congress had recently convened in Philadelphia. Ever since General Gage arrived in Boston with three thousand troops to impose Parliament's will upon the colonists, Boston became the heart of the resistance movement. There was great tension in the air fueling a rising discontent among the citizenry. Aid in the form of firewood, clothing, and foodstuffs of every description was routed to the besieged Bostonians by patriots all across the hemisphere.

Drew was immediately invited to the Captain's quarters. The congenial captain pointed to a chair beside a small table filled with charts and maps.

"Thanks, Captain Jones," Drew said, taking a seat.

"I'd like to share some sweet cider from my own orchard with you, Drew. Tea is poison to us now," Captain Jones placed a tankard and two tin mugs on the table.

"Thank you, Sir. My father's orchards have not yet produced a heavy crop of apples. Cider is my favorite drink. I hope to purchase a few gallons for the tavern."

The captain poured their cider and took a seat next to him. "I'm not sure that Portsmouth is a good place to visit right now, Lad."

"Why, Captain?"

"I was in Newburyport not very far from Boston a couple of days ago to take on a cargo of pork and beef. It seems that General Gage and his British troops plan to check every town where the patriots may be hiding gun powder and military stores. The story traveling rapidly through the local grapevine is that the Royal Navy has been ordered to secure the powder and other stores at Fort William and Mary on the Piscataqua River."

Drew was alarmed by the news. "Does that mean you may not be able to drop me off and pick up my supplies on your return trip, Captain?"

"The Royal Navy has nothing on me, lad. I'll drop you off as planned. We just have to make sure we have nothing illegal in our holds. They'll board us if they are at Portsmouth. The ships most likely will have a contingent of Royal Marines on board. Be careful who you talk to and what you say once you're ashore."

Drew thought about the statement for a few seconds. "Well, most of my stuff is food and drink. I was also going to ask Daniel Cullen, an old friend of the family, for extra paper and ink for our new school on the Kennebec."

"I know Daniel Cullen very well. His paper, the *COASTAL BEACON,* is very critical of the British, especially General Gage. His wife is a native lady of renowned beauty."

"Mrs. Cullen and my mother are good friends," Drew proudly told him.

Captain Jones' prophetic caution was good advice. Just as soon as the sleek schooner tacked to enter the Piscataqua River, a British warship with all guns manned followed them upstream. Jones continued with full sail up to the large commercial wharf at Portsmouth where he gently slid to a stop at the most northern point on the dock. The British ship did the same immediately behind him. A large contingent of marines rushed down the gangplank to secure the wharf. A troop of marines was instantly ordered to board the schooner and to inspect for contraband.

Drew casually stepped off the schooner and walked toward the large concentration of warehouses that dominated the riverside. No one bothered him. He turned to see that the marines were combing every square foot of Captain Jones' ship and entered the largest warehouse owned by a prominent businessman, John Langdon. Drew normally purchased most of his supplies from the Langdon facility. The moment he entered the warehouse, he felt a tense atmosphere among the workers who were traditionally jovial and helpful. Today there was no hearty welcome to accept his business. He looked over several bags of potatoes, apples, coffee beans and barrels of molasses before he stepped up to the counter to place his order.

Suddenly, the stillness that had permeated the warehouse was shattered by a squad of British marines who entered the building by smashing the door down instead of lifting the string for the latch. "We have nothing to hide," exclaimed the elderly manager of the warehouse.

"We'll determine that," explained a sergeant in charge of the squad. "We have information that your company was involved in stealing powder and arms from Fort William and Mary. If it's here, we'll find it."

The manager sighed and turned to Drew. "They won't find anything. What can I do for you, Mr. LeClair?"

Drew handed him a list for supplies. "Can you have our order ready to place on Captain Jones' ship as soon as possible?"

"Yes, the quicker you get out of Portsmouth the better. We'll fill your order shortly. We're a little short of candles, but we have everything else. Tell Captain Jones to remain at his berth," the clerk nervously replied.

Drew paid the man with gold coins and left the warehouse to visit Daniel Cullen's office for the COASTAL BEACON a short distance north up the river. Mr. Cullen was not in, but his foreman told Drew that several reams of paper and a few gallons of ink made from linseed oil and lamp black were put to one side for the new school. The three men in the composing room volunteered to transport the ink and paper to the ship.

122

Back at the ship, Captain Jones had originally intended to return to Newburyport, but with so much Royal Navy activity about, he was anxious to leave the area on the next out-going tide. He hoped to deliver Drew and his supplies up the Kennebec before nightfall. It was a prudent move with the Royal Navy on the rampage.

Once they were underway, and had cleared the mouth of the Piscataqua River, Captain Jones and Drew sat in his quarters reading the latest copy of the *COASTAL BEACON*. The headlines for the main article shattered their composure:

**Unknown persons have taken powder and arms from Fort William and Mary by force of arms.**

Governor John Wentworth has declared a state of emergency for the city of Portsmouth placing it under martial law. General Gage ordered troops from Boston into the city hoping to retrieve the confiscated powder. Those responsible for the crime will be diligently sought and brought to justice, declared the Governor.

The act of war may be the opening salvo of the conflict that an indifferent Parliament has contributed to. An insurrection has slowly been taking place in the thirteen colonies for several years. Supplications to the Crown for justice have been callously ignored, leaving their colonial brothers with no other outlet than to protest in any way possible.

A dark curtain is descending upon the land. If a benevolent and caring Parliament is truly seeking to resolve problems, then their brothers in the colonies are willing, even eager, to meet them halfway. A serious challenge has been issued. How does the Crown respond to our plea for recognition?

Drew returned home a different and more sober human being. He had seen firsthand how the British treated the population. Everyone he had talked to in Portsmouth believed that armed resistance and open conflict were imminent. That first night of his return he and his father were sitting in front of the snapping fireplace in the tavern. Abel filled his pipe and lit it from a firebrand in the fireplace.

"You want to be careful burning hemlock wood. It snaps and sends sparks out on the floor, Drew."

Drew shook his head in agreement. "If trouble begins, where do you think it will start, Father?"

"Boston has been besieged by the British, and our colonial militias have formed a partial ring around the city. If war breaks out it will start there. They're too arrogant and greedy to let the colonists have their way. Once it starts, it will be a vicious fight. I'm not so sure about my role in a conflict. I have much experience that could benefit the colonists. I'd like to contribute to our struggle for freedom."

Drew knew what was in his father's heart. "You've seen enough combat, Father. Mother needs you here at home. To be honest, I've been thinking about joining the local militia unit. However, I could not leave unless you and mother agreed to care for little Abel. Ben would also need some assistance running the inn and tavern," Drew replied, shaking his head.

"You know we would be pleased to do that, Drew. I'd rather go myself than to see you leave us," Abel stared into the reaching flames. "For now, we should prepare for the winter months and be ready to do our duty, whatever it is, when that time comes."

A few months after their return from Portsmouth, Captain Jones tied his schooner up to the LeClair dock, prepared to stay for the night. He seemed ill at ease and unsure about himself. His normal jovial disposition was replaced by a stern seriousness.

Drew was the first to confront the Captain who had become a close friend of the family. "Captain Jones, do I detect something wrong? If so, forgive my boldness."

The sailor sipped his mug of coffee and looked into the eyes of Abel and Drew. The flickering shadows from the fire highlighted the lines around his mouth. "You are an observant lad. Yes, I have something on my mind that has troubled me and given me much concern. I'm turning to you for help." The Captain watched the flames leaping up into the chimney for several seconds and continued. "My dear sister passed away recently leaving her daughter alone. My precious Annabelle Meyers has been a wonderful addition to my household. For the past few weeks I've been blessed by her presence at my small home in Machias. In order to make a living, I must be away from home for weeks at a time. I don't want to take Ana with me now that the seas are more dangerous than ever for colonial merchants. I've been wondering if you might have a place for Ana to stay and work while I'm away? She's a wonderful young lady, and I love her dearly. It's almost as if my wife, Anna, was still with me."

Abel was quick to reply. "Captain Jones, be assured that we would welcome your niece to our establishment. We have a need for another pair of hands and would be willing to pay good wages for her assistance."

"I knew I came to the right place," Captain Jones smiled. "Ana is on the schooner in my quarters. She was too shy to ask you herself."

"Drew," said his father, "go out and welcome the young lady to our home. You should have brought her in, Captain. It's cold out there tonight."

Drew walked down the path to the schooner holding a lantern to see the gangplank. "Ahoy there, Ana. Your uncle wants you to come into the tavern. I'm Drew LeClair."

A voice answered from the small room on the quarterdeck. "I hear you. I'm Annabelle Meyers, Captain Jones' niece," she replied, adjusting to the limited light.

Drew held the lantern so that the lady could pick her way to the gangplank. "Brrr, it is cold out tonight," she said, stepping lightly onto the dock. "I don't want to be a nuisance to anyone."

"Your uncle is very proud of you. May I call you Ana?"

"Please do," she grinned. "May I have the same privilege and call you Drew? I've heard my uncle mention you often."

Drew guided her up the banking to the tavern, opening the front door for her to enter.

"Ah, here's my Ana," cried Captain Jones. "Come, my dear, sit beside me. This gentleman across the table from me is Drew's father, Abel LeClair. He has offered you a job and a place to stay here at the inn and tavern while I'm at sea. What do you think?"

Ana was a young lady about twenty years old. She was dressed in a warm woolen dress with a flax shawl around her shoulders and a white bonnet on her head. Her coal black hair hung loose about her shoulders. She was slightly apprehensive being in the room with strangers even if they were friends of her uncle. She quickly backed up to the fireplace to warm herself and slowly swept the room with her dark brown eyes, appraising Drew and his father for several seconds before answering her Uncle Samuel.

"My Uncle Samuel has often spoken about your family here on the Kennebec. Even though we've never met, I feel as if I know you. I'm willing to work for my keep. I can read and write English thanks to my dear mother who taught me. I was able to teach young students to do the same in a small school recently opened at Machias for two years until my mother became sick. I took care of her until the end came. I promise to work hard to earn your trust and respect, and I thank you for being so generous."

Abel smiled, liking the young lady's direct mannerism. "The LeClair family sincerely welcomes you to our home and hearth. I speak for my son, Drew, my three year old grandson, Abel, Jr., and my dear wife, Marie. We are fortunate to have you. Our business has grown, and we do need another helping hand. May I call you Ana?"

She smiled. The father sounded exactly like his son, Drew. "Of course, Mr. LeClair. You should also know that two years ago I lost my dear husband who drowned in a severe storm at sea."

"I remember your uncle told me about that terrible tragedy," Drew mentioned. "Please sit at the table while I get you some hot coffee and some of our delicious apple pie."

"Thank you. I am hungry."

That evening, Captain Jones brought them up to date on current events. "I'm not surprised to hear about the tension that exists," he said, smoking his clay pipe. "I was at a meeting with some of our local patriots when the Royal Navy entered our harbor with a demand that we tear down the liberty pole we had erected in the center of town. The people were infuriated by their arrogance and airs of superiority…"

Captain Jones went on to tell them that a close friend who commanded a sloop called *Unity* attacked the British man-of-war *Margarita* with the loss of twenty men on each side. The decks of both vessels were literally drenched with blood. Eventually, at great cost, the men from *Machias* were able to capture the *Margarita.* They sailed it out into the Atlantic flying a flag of Maine with a green white pine tree on the topsail of the ship, intent on raiding British ships that sailed the Atlantic coast.

Abel and Drew sat mesmerized by the Captain's tale of horror. Every man in the colonies at that historic moment in time was doing a lot of soul-searching, seeking an answer to the question "where do we go from here?" Abel and Drew were in that same situation. Abel was afraid that Drew would volunteer to join Captain Jones who had confided with them that he was going to turn his schooner into a privateer in search of heavily loaded British ships. If the colonies declared war against their motherland, they would need all the food, clothing, and arms the daring privateers could capture from their enemy.

That night Drew was determined to be a part of the resistance to the brutal tactics of the British. It was not a question, it was simply a matter of when and how he could contribute. People of the land were rising to defend their rights as free men…

# Chapter Seventeen

The next day, Captain Jones was up early to take advantage of the out-going tide. He had accomplished his mission to establish his niece, Ana, at a safe place with people he trusted and respected while the outside world was tearing itself apart. Drew and Ana stood on the dock watching the sleek schooner being swept into the center of the stream. Captain Jones waved a final farewell to them and turned his attention to guiding the sleek craft downstream. Drew had seen a more determined and reticent Captain Samuel Jones that morning. They had talked quietly over oatmeal and coffee. Their last few words worried his young friend. When they were alone, Drew had asked him what his plans were.

He was reluctant to share his intentions. "The simple answer to your question, lad, is I really don't know for certain. I'm returning to Machias to take on additional supplies and a couple more men for an extended stay at sea. We had removed some small swivel cannons from the British ship, *Margarita*. I plan to attach one aft, one forward, on the port and on the starboard. They will make our mission of disrupting British shipping a little easier and will prevent confrontations from getting out of hand.

"Don't worry about me. Thank your family for taking Ana in. I plan to go in harm's way to deliver as much trouble to the British as my small schooner is capable of doing. I can outrun any man-of-war afloat. However, those slow lumbering freighters are fair game. They'll soon know that we intend to fight for our liberties. I'm a seaman, so my contribution will be made on the ocean, not on the land."

"May God be with you, Captain Jones," Drew had replied, embracing the stalwart patriot.

Ana quietly stood on the LeClair dock staring at the schooner on its way out to sea until it disappeared around the bend. She bravely fought the tears that formed in her dark brown eyes. She had a terrible premonition that she was seeing her uncle for the last time. A silent sigh passed her lips as she asked God to watch over the last blood relative she had on this earth.

"There goes a very brave Patriot," Drew exclaimed, caught up in the emotional intensity of the moment. "I hope his passion to close with the enemy does not override his good judgment. I'll miss him. He has been such a good friend to me and my family."

Ana was pleased to hear that. "He has always been a cautious man with common sense. I love him dearly for his gentle ways. He has been kind and thoughtful to my mother and me, especially after my husband was lost at sea. The deep and dark Atlantic swallowed him one day, and now it's as if he had never existed. All that is left for us are the memories. The cold waters of the Atlantic jealously guard its secrets, divulging them to no man."

"I'm sorry for your loss, Ana. I understand what it means to lose a soul mate," Drew told her. "The only consolation is that little Abel, Jr., helps to brighten my days."

"He's a wonderful child. You're truly blessed," she replied, wiping the tears from her eyes. "Come, we should return to the tavern. Your mother is going to show me how they make the apple pies your tavern is so famous for."

Captain Jones had left a few copies of the current *COASTAL BEACON* at the tavern. Drew made it a point of reviewing it when they got back to the tavern and was surprised to learn that a Colonel Benedict Arnold from Connecticut and Colonel Ethan Allen from Vermont had captured Fort Ticonderoga from the British. The capture with no losses from either side was a great victory for the colonies, producing large numbers of cannons, mortars, and gun powder. The Continental Army was lacking any such inventory of artillery.

Shortly after the capture of Ticonderoga, Arnold launched an attack against Fort Frederick at Crown Point, several miles north of Ticonderoga on Lake Champlain, without losing a soldier. This daring capture of the two forts at the southern end of Champlain gave the Patriots control of the Hudson Valley-Lake Champlain corridor, successfully blocking any assault from the north to isolate New England from the other colonies. If that was accomplished, the British could consolidate their forces to defeat the patriots one colony at a time.

On April nineteenth, an exchange of fire and the ensuing losses on both sides took place at a small bridge near Lexington and Concord, Massachusetts. British troops had left Boston to destroy potential arms stored in the area the same as when they established martial law in Portsmouth, New Hampshire. At the Concord Bridge the British regulars and marines were confronted by the minute men militias from Massachusetts. A lone unknown musket shot turned the confrontation into a blood bath. The militia retreated from the roadway at the bridge. The British quickly retraced their steps back to Boston in a withering fusillade lurking behind the stone walls and forests along the roadway. The British suffered heavy losses during their retreat to the city.

The following statement in the paper caught everyone's attention:

> *June 16, 1775. A furious battle is taking place in Boston as this paper is being printed… The country is formally at war with Great Britain.*

The last statement was a sobering fact to every family in the country. War, with all of its horror and sacrifices, was now a part of their daily lives! Drew stared at the flames in the fireplace for several minutes. He knew from Captain Jones about the battle for Bunker Hill in Charlestown. The Continental Congress had appointed General George Washington to be Commander-in-Chief of the Continental Army. He had arrived in Boston to take over the militia that had laid siege on the city of Boston.

Money for equipment, supplies and manpower was meager or nonexistent. The first campaign that General Washington ordered was a two-pronged attack against Canada with the chance their northern neighbor might join their southern brothers to repel the British. He visualized the assault to be widely welcomed by the people of Canada. There were high hopes within the new Continental Army for a successful campaign. The commander of troops in Quebec was British General Carleton who had recently sent half of his troops to Boston, leaving fewer troops to defend Quebec on the St. Lawrence River.

One force under Philip Schuyler was sent to secure Montreal. He became ill and General Richard Montgomery replaced him. The plan called for Montgomery to rapidly drive toward Quebec to supplement Benedict Arnold's attack up the Kennebec River through the Maine wilderness toward Quebec. Colonel Arnold had collected 1100 men and left Newburyport in Massachusetts arriving at the mouth of the Kennebec on September 19th. He stopped briefly with his armada at the Jackson Warehouse before continuing up the river as far as Gardner. Colonel Arnold established a command post and staging area at the old Fort Western barracks building.

Tempo on the Kennebec increased. A steady stream of schooners and lighter sail ships carrying men and supplies traversed the mighty Kennebec. The Coburn boatyard had a contract to build several hundred flat-bottomed boats for the force. They were constructed of green wood weighing over four hundred pounds, and were capable of carrying four to six men and their equipment.

The route north to Quebec from Fort Western included some of the most desolate landscapes in the country, especially during the winter months. Dark forests surrounded by large areas of swampland would test the army's endurance to the limit. Sheer exhaustion, hunger, and bone-chilling cold would haunt every hour of their advance. The heavy boats being dragged over numerous portages would be the supreme test of Arnold's leadership skill.

Washington had already sent a message to Canada beseeching them to join the patriots in the thirteen colonies: "We have taken up arms in defense of our liberty, our property, and our wives and children. We are determined to preserve them or die. Come then, my brethren. Let us run together to the same goal... Tyranny will never be able to prevail." Washington also ordered the troops to observe strict discipline and good order, especially towards their contact with Canadians.

The Coburn Boatyard was filled with activity. The boats were leaving the yard as the men began to arrive. Drew had taken over much of his father's duties on the ferry while his father worked at the boatyard to help fill the rush order for boats. The Kennebec had never been as busy. Boats filled to the limit with supplies for the expedition made a single file heading north on the incoming tide.

Little Abel roamed freely about the tavern. He was an energetic five year old that had won everybody's heart, especially his dad's. His grandmother LeClair was more lenient with him than his father. He had taken a liking to Ana who worked long hours in the tavern. Abel, Jr., called her Aunt Ana.

One day, Drew and his father had talked with Colonel Arnold at the boatyard. When the Colonel learned that Drew and Amelia had made a trip to Canada over the same route he anticipated to use to Quebec, he offered to hire Drew as a civilian guide for the expedition. Drew was quick to remind him that it was a difficult route to Quebec with the prospect of winter not far away. Winters were long and severe, and the further north the force advanced, the more severe they became. If the troops were not prepared for the deep snows and cold temperatures they would perish either from the cold or from starvation. Hauling and lugging the loaded boats through extensive marshlands would be a daunting task. The numerous portages were not impossible, but they would slow the formation down to a crawl. Game was almost nonexistent, so food would have to be carried from Fort Western.

Drew also informed Arnold that the northern portions of the route past the Dead River and Chaudiere Lake to the Chaudiere River were the easiest section provided the waterways were not frozen. Fish was available in those waters.

Colonel Arnold listened carefully to Drew. "The situation is graver than I had been led to believe."

"It's slightly under two hundred miles from Western to Quebec City, Sir," Drew added soberly.

"Irrespective of how difficult the journey will be, we are committed to the mission, and I plan to carry out my orders. Can I depend on your expertise as a guide with the advance party of soldiers?" the Colonel asked gravely.

"I'll have to think about the offer, Sir," Drew replied.

"May I remind you, Colonel Arnold," Abel said. "I speak as an experienced soldier in the French Army. Your decision to attack Canada may be more successful if you carried your force around the Gaspe and up the St. Lawrence River by ship. The men would arrive at the point of intense combat in excellent physical condition. Numerous small ships such as armed schooners are available for transport."

The Colonel frowned on the suggestion. "My orders are explicit. You must know what orders mean to a soldier."

"That's a given, Sir. I was merely voicing an opinion. Any officer has an obligation to evaluate every possible means of carrying out his orders. It's very likely that you will arrive at Quebec via the Kennebec with fewer men you can use in besieging the city. The salt water route would give you one hundred percent of your force. I understand that the decision is yours. My son will give you his answer shortly."

"Thank you for this informative visit, Mr. LeClair. Your suggestion is a valid option, but we do not have one gunship available for our use. The Royal Navy has a large presence in the northern waters that we could never counter. I'll look forward to your son's decision."

That evening at the tavern, the LeClair family sat around the fireplace to discuss the future. Drew's mother was opposed to his leaving on such a trip in the early stages of winter. "Harsh winters come early that far north, my son."

"I know, Mother," he replied. "I'm not concerned about the difficulty of the trip. "I've been wanting to contribute in some way to the struggle that is raging around us. I know it would be a burden on all of you. Little Abel requires a lot of care. It may sound selfish, but I'm inclined to accept Colonel Arnold's offer."

His father understood his desire to do something of value to the campaign. "I have the same longing, son. You're a logical choice to act as a guide for the expedition; there's no question about that. If it's successful, it could mean the difference between victory and failure. Either way, you'll have some tales to tell your son and grandchildren."

Ana had sat quietly listening to the conversation as was her way. "If you do go, Drew, do not worry about little Abel. I'm willing to help with the chores and with caring for your son. This same conversation is taking place in homes throughout the colonies. My Uncle had a similar one in Machias before he made the decision to go to sea. He was anxious to contribute to the effort to free the colonies from the tyranny the English have imposed on us. If we do not react to unjust laws and taxation, what do we become?"

"You speak with wisdom, Ana," Abel replied. "To do nothing is to submit to the tyranny. If I was a younger man, I'd find it hard to leave my beloved family, but it would be their safety and welfare that would motivate me to join against the mother country."

Drew looked around the table at those he loved dearly. His father and Ana had said it all. "Most of the officers and men have already arrived at Fort Western. Arnold is stockpiling a tremendous amount of food."

"I still have some doubts about any military expedition or political conversations having any success in bringing Canada to fight against the British," Abel added. "I could be wrong, but we can pray for success."

That evening, Drew made up his mind to send a notice to Colonel Arnold the next morning that he accepted the position as a scout for the Canada expedition. In the meantime, he had to assemble his personal items for the trip and attend to private affairs in preparation for a prolonged absence.

Two days later, Drew said good-bye to his family. Over the years, he had gone away from home to sea several times. This parting was different. He was volunteering as an active participant in a military campaign heading north with winter not far away. He silently prayed that his father's assessment of the endeavor was incorrect. Before Drew crossed the river, he paid a visit to see Pru. He approached the trading post, noting the white smoke curling from the chimney. Pru saw him as she was getting an armful of firewood.

"Hello, Pru," Drew hailed her from a distance.

She dropped the wood and ran to him. "It's so nice to see you, Drew. Father has left for Fort Western."

"I've come to say good-bye, Pru. I'm on my way to volunteer myself as a scout for the Quebec expedition. Have you heard from Joseph?" he asked, knowing that her husband had sought sanctuary somewhere further north in Maine at a Tory stronghold.

"Nothing, Drew," she sighed, taking his arm in hers, leading him to the trading post. "He left me and Pearl without a word. I guess I expected more from him than he was able to deliver. At one time I loved him. Now it has turned to anger and disgust. He was never the man I thought he was, but enough about him. Your family and friends will miss you. I'll pray for your safe return to us. Would you like a cup of hot tea or coffee?"

"I've already eaten a hearty breakfast at the tavern, Pru, but a hot tea will taste good, the evil drink that it is."

"Ah, it tastes better when it comes from the Caribbean duty free," she smiled.

Drew sat at a chair next to the fireplace, removing his pack and coat. She served them two cups of steaming hot tea. "You and I go back a long ways, Pru. How differently things turned out for both of us."

"If I had the chance, I'd do things differently," she quickly replied.

"Pru, every person alive could say that. I want to ask you a question. You don't have to answer it, but I've given it a lot of thought."

"Ask your question, Drew."

"Is it possible that Thomas would take up arms against the colonists? The thought that I might face him as an adversary in combat frightens me. I'm not sure what my reaction would be."

"Dear friend," Pru exclaimed, placing a hand on his arm. "If Thomas is low enough to turn against his friends and neighbors, then he deserves what he gets. He's cruel and is capable of anything. I'm having our marriage annulled on the basis of abandonment of Pearl and myself. I hate him for his cowardice."

Drew was surprised to hear Pru speak so viciously about the man she had married. "Your description of him is accurate. I wish you luck, old friend. I should be on my way," he said, finishing his tea.

She rose with him. "You'll never know how much I hate to see you leave, Drew. My prayers seem inadequate." She was having difficulty hiding the tears that filled her eyes.

"Thanks for the support," he replied, taking her into his arms. "You deserved better than Thomas, Pru."

She clung to his embrace and lifted her lips to meet his. She wept in his comforting arms. "Good-bye, Drew. Come back to us. May the north star guide your travels."

It was difficult for him to leave. She remained silent as he turned to walk away. They both thought of earlier times when life was simple and filled with promise. Now, uncertainty filled the air and, tomorrow was not a guarantee. He waved one last time. She returned it with tears blinding her vision of him.

Drew hailed a schooner that had tied up on the opposite shore for the evening for a lift to Fort Western, and ran to catch his father's ferry across the river. His farewell with his father was filled with emotion. Abel knew from experience the trials ahead of his son. "Do not worry about me, Father. I'll do my best. Thanks for caring for little Abel, your namesake."

"You know it's not a chore but a pleasure, Son," Abel told him with a strained voice. "I expect that this expedition will be long and difficult. All wars and conflicts are fought by a select few for the benefit of the masses. The soldier's lot is not an easy one. My only advice to you is to follow your instincts. They'll serve you well. Watch your backside and keep your powder dry, and when that little voice inside of you speaks, listen to it. Never forget that you are loved by many people. I'm so proud of you, Drew."

With those few words, Drew hugged his father and jumped off the ferry at a run.

# Chapter Eighteen

Drew arrived at the large building within the Fort Western compound with the same canoe he and Amelia had used for the trip to Canada. He had hooked a ride up to Gardner with a schooner and rode the canoe up to the fort. He calculated that it would be perfect for him guiding the expedition. He secured the canoe to a balsam fir tree and strapped on his backpack. He did not trust his personal belongings unattended with such a large group of men. The fort was a beehive of activity.

"Where can I find Colonel Arnold?" Drew asked of a young soldier sitting on the bank of the river.

The soldier pointed to a large pile of supplies that had just been unloaded. "He's that man with the hat beside the barrels of food."

"Thanks," Drew answered, recognizing Colonel Arnold.

A tall, heavy built man with long hair dressed in a deerskin hunting shirt was having a discussion with Arnold. "Hell, Colonel, none of my men would think of serving under anyone besides me. Their loyalty is more to me than the cause."

Drew overheard some of the discussion and announced himself, "Excuse me, Sir."

Arnold turned to face Drew. "Yes, young man?"

"I'm Drew LeClair, Sir. I'm here to accept your offer to lead the expedition to Quebec."

"Now I remember you." Arnold recalled their conversation. "You've made my day, Drew LeClair. This is Captain Daniel Morgan. He commands a company of Virginians. I plan to use his company as the vanguard for the expedition. You two will have plenty of time to get acquainted."

Daniel Morgan offered Drew his hand. It was the largest hand Drew had shaken. "I'm glad to meet you, Drew LeClair. That carbine you're carrying looks like a fine weapon."

Drew smiled at his observation. "My father had it made for me several years ago when this territory was alive with rampaging Abenaki and French Jesuit priests. The carbine has a rifled barrel making it capable of accurately shooting much farther than the British Brown Bess. My father was a sergeant in the French Marines until he was wounded in the leg. He taught me to load, aim, and shoot three rounds a minute. I told him it was impossible, but he persisted, and with much practice, I was able to do it."

"Your father sounds like my kind of sergeant," Daniel laughed heartily. He had a booming voice that carried far. "Tell me, when was the last time you followed the proposed route to Quebec?"

"It was about three years ago, Sir. I traveled it with the lady who became my wife. We went as far as Sartigan in Canada. She was a Penacook Indian maiden who had used the trails many times over the years. It was the main trail for most of the Indians in the area."

"What happen to your wife?" Colonel Arnold asked.

"She died from smallpox," Drew answered.

"I'm sorry for you," Arnold replied. "What do you think about the route?"

"The route will be a difficult one for an armed force who has to carry munitions and foodstuff the full distance. I would not call it impossible, but it will be a heavy drain on the men's endurance. I have a modified canoe for my personal use. It has a hide covering that has been strengthened and waterproofed by several layers of shellac. Dragging it over the portages and the swampy lands is much easier than the large boats made at the Coburn Boatyard. Do you have any instructions for me, Colonel Arnold?"

"I am starting an advance party to move food and medical supplies north in case they are needed. I want to stage as much as possible to ensure our food supply. Would you be interested in leading them as far forward as possible?" Arnold asked, liking what he saw in Drew.

"I'm prepared to leave anytime. If you'll direct me to the crews in the advance party, I'll introduce myself to them. Now, I have some personal food supplies in my pack. I prefer to hold these in reserve until we get to the Dead River area. Until then, I'll share the rations you provide."

"Sounds like a sensible plan." Colonel Arnold pointed to a party of men loading supplies onto several boats tied up at the waterfront. "Captain Morgan is also sending a small detachment with this group. You are primarily responsible to me, but you should work with all of the advance parties with a spirit of cooperation. Is that understood?"

"That was my intention, Colonel."

"I think we'll hit it off, LeClair. I'm glad to have you aboard." Daniel Morgan told him.

With that, Drew headed towards the riverside. He told the men in the supply party that their first obstacle would be the falls at the old Fort Halifax known as Ticonic Falls. The next portage was at Skowhegan about forty miles upriver. Many of the volunteers were younger than Drew's thirty-one years. He introduced himself and mentioned that ropes were useful to haul the boats around obstacles, and even in the water they could make better time dragging them from the land with ropes. He explained that between Fort Western and the Great Carrying Place there were four falls to be by-passed, and many rapids to be avoided.

Captain Daniel Morgan and a squad of six men joined the advance party for security. He met Drew at the river before they left Fort Western. "May I call you Drew?" he asked.

"Of course, if I may call you Daniel."

"Do you want me to send one of my men with you? I suggest that you work ahead of our slower supply column, marking the way when it may be in doubt. I like your hide canoe."

"Thanks just the same. I prefer to be alone in the canoe. I'll leave blazes on trees whenever the proper route seems doubtful. If you don't mind I'll help myself to some of your tea, flour and pork. I'll wait for you at the old Fort Halifax ruins. It has no value for the present. For your information, there is nothing in the Maine woods that can harm you. No poisonous snakes or vicious animals. You may meet an occasional Native American. They will be harmless. I'll guarantee that. The Abenaki are going to remain neutral during this struggle between white men. I plan to leave here shortly so that I can scout for unusual obstacles. The old fort is about a day's travel from here."

"Good luck, Drew. We'll meet again soon," Daniel laughed and turned away.

Drew was glad to get underway. He was anxious to check for potential problem spots. The colorful spectacle of fall foliage in full bloom was a time when he enjoyed the forest the most. It gave him a melancholic feeling. The bright colors celebrated the death of summer and the birth of the harsh winter months ahead. The solitude of the forest enriched his soul.

The wilderness guards its secrets with silence. Epic tales of love, life and mystery lie buried in the rock-strewn soil. Drew often wondered what tales could be told if the forest could talk. Those adventures it has collected over the centuries are held in bondage caressed by the north wind as it passes through the canopies, carrying the secrets to eternity.

At night, the North Star is ever so faithful in displaying its brilliance for all the world to see. It stands in the heavens unfailingly in the same location. It is the only star in the galaxy that remains above the northern pole axis. It has guided forest travelers on their journey ever since man roamed the vast earth in search of their own destiny. Those who lived out their hopes and dreams and accomplishments under the wooded canopies have all faded away without our knowing who they were. There are those who claim to hear the silent cries of the long dead, but to most there is only the haunting howl of the wind whistling through the branches reaching to the heavens.

Drew contemplated his Native American legacy from his mother. He had always felt a strong kinship with the land, be they primeval forests or the vast ocean waters he had sailed on. It was a feeling of belonging that made him comfortable and at ease with his place. It was impossible for him not to think of his beloved Amelia. Memories and images of their time together on their trip to Sartigan blazed anew in his heart and he was lonely again.

Helping Colonel Arnold to bring an armed force through the wilderness to Quebec gave him a sense of accomplishment. He was able to contribute to the cause of liberty. It was a fight they had to win. His mother and father had worked tirelessly to carve a future out of the soil of Acadia, and on the Kennebec. The possibility that they might not survive another eviction by the English was wearing on them.

The Ticonic Falls was the first portage on the river from Fort Western. Drew had met Daniel Morgan's advance party at the falls a short ways from the old Fort Halifax ruins and pushed on to Skowhegan Falls. This was a location rich with memories for Drew. He relived the moments he and Amelia had spent on the flat island above the falls. Skowhegan Falls was the last organized town on the Kennebec River. From that point north, the primeval forest would be their host until they reached Sartigan, the first French settlement in Canada. Getting around the first couple of falls was to be repeated several times as they journeyed to the north, each one becoming harder and more difficult than the previous portage.

That evening at Skowhegan Falls, Drew shared some of his memories with Daniel Morgan over a campfire before they turned in for the night. Morgan had a rough exterior and was boisterous on occasion. Drew found him to be a good listener and a caring soul. He was a born leader. The men in his company worshipped him and enthusiastically followed him. They were the best disciplined company in Arnold's brigade. The vast wilderness cultivated a sense of brotherhood and responsibility toward each other that was lacking in general society.

Daniel had told Drew that night that he had received a message from a runner that Colonel Arnold had left Fort Western in a canoe with an Indian as a guide. They were now a force stretched out for miles along the Kennebec. Daniel mentioned that any orders for the vanguard units would come to him via the Indian guides Arnold had hired to dispatch messages.

About twelve miles from the Skowhegan Falls, there was another portage called Norridgewook Falls. It had been an important Indian village with remnants of a Catholic Church still standing. Drew passed it, dragging his light canoe around the falls and continued his journey north. He was alert and observant of everything before him. Whenever a brook or a trickle of water deviated from the main water body, he left noticeable blaze marks on trees to indicate the proper route.

Always in the back of his mind were memories of Amelia as she had been on that trip they took together. It had been a time of discovery that proved to be right for the couple. Her loss still traumatized him. Their time together had been so short. He was thankful for that time, but it did not curb the yearning he still harbored for her.

During the long journey to Quebec, Drew made up his mind that he would join Morgan's company of riflemen. Once they arrived at Quebec, his services were no longer needed, and he could revert to being a soldier in the attack on the city. When he discussed that with Daniel, he had affectionately slapped him on the shoulder and told him he'd be proud to have him in the company.

The numerous falls and other obstacles on the river demanded that the heavy boats filled with supplies and equipment had to be dragged or lifted by hand around the obstruction. It was tiring work that taxed many of the men who became ill. Not only was it grueling work, it was extremely slow, and winter was on its way! The heavy exertions demanded adequate nutrition and the men were ravenous all the time. Starvation was not far away. Much food was lost trying to manhandle the boats around falls. Many of the boats leaked badly, contaminating much of the foodstuff.

The great carrying place was a most strenuous ordeal. The boats had to be dragged or carried twelve miles through marshland to connect to the Dead River, leaving the Kennebec to continue to Moosehead Lake. Several boats had been lost during this transfer from one river to another. Hunger was so rampant that many men boiled tallow candles in water to make a hot gruel to drink. The colorful foliage had disappeared by the time they reached the carrying place, and the nights were getting increasingly colder. Several men deserted and made their way back down the Kennebec. The prospect of starvation or freezing to death was beyond what some men were capable of handling. For the remaining men, the hope of finding food and some shelter as they came closer to Canada was all that kept them moving. The French settlements were believed to be sympathetic to the cause of the Continental Army.

The small amount of pemmican Drew had carried with him in his pack was already consumed. His mother had made up some food bars about six inches long for the journey made from barley grain, hazel nuts, honey, dried apple pieces, and smoked pieces of venison. She had then baked them until they were crunchy like a hard cracker. They were tasty, nourishing and light to carry in the forest. He still had about twenty bars left in his pack. The food in Arnold's commissary was dangerously low. Consequently Drew and the Virginia Company were ordered to act as hunters and foragers.

Daniel was pulling his canoe over some rapids when he stopped and pointed to a doe standing next to the marshland ahead of them. "Can you see that deer, Drew?"

Drew followed his arm. "Yes, I see it. That's a long shot, Daniel."

"My Kentucky musket will not reach that far. Try it, Drew. The men desperately need food," Daniel replied, kneeling in front of Drew. "Here, use my shoulder to steady your aim."

"I usually use maximum loads," Drew said, checking the pan for powder. "Steady now, Daniel. Hold your breath and plug your ears."

Drew placed the muzzle of his carbine on Daniel's massive shoulder and dropped to a kneeling position. He knew how important this deer was to the hungry men. Gripping his faithful carbine in his strong hands, Drew checked for wind, took aim, and slowly squeezed the trigger. The deer dropped as his heavy slug knocked it to the ground.

"Good shot!" Daniel screamed, turning to two of his men. "Cross that marsh and get that deer. The rest of you get a fire going. We're going to make a venison stew. I've got a few potatoes in my sack, and there's a small package of rice in one of the boats. We feast tonight."

That evening was a welcome pause in the slow march north. Daniel shared some of his knowledge of the trail with the men. They were encouraged that it would be easier traveling once they got to Dead River. That waterway was more like a canal than a stream. Granite ledges were several feet high on both sides where the water had carved a channel through the granite over the years. There was some possibility that fish would be available too.

The need for food replenishment was desperate. Survival was in question at this juncture of the expedition's progress. Drew maintained his position at the head of the force while Morgan's men became hunters and foragers with meager success. The forest in that area seemed empty of animals of any type. There were a few falls on the Dead River, but primarily it was an easy segment of the trail to make up for lost time. Off to the south and west, the massive Bigelow Mountains stood like sentinels looking down on their arduous journey.

Many of the men complained that they would never have signed on for the campaign if they had known how difficult it would be. Drew had warned Colonel Arnold, but he had dismissed it. A good night's sleep could restore tired and aching muscles, but an empty stomach had no such easy cure; it needed nourishment. The fact was the men were starving.

Shortly after the arrival of the column on the Dead River, they were hit by a furious hurricane that completely flooded the area for miles around the normal river channel. The flood obliterated all of the landmarks, presenting a problem to Drew. The night the storm hit he hunkered down wrapped in his doeskin with the canoe on top of him. It was a long desolate night. He would need something to orient the long column of desperate men. He prayed for guidance. In the middle of the night the storm calmed so that he could see stars. He quickly located the North Star. If he followed that course he knew it would lead to the Chaudiere Pond and adjacent Chaudiere River that emptied into the Saint Lawrence River. He turned the canoe so that it pointed north. The North Star never failed the wilderness traveler. It never moved from its position.

When Drew saw a stand of large balsam fir trees, he stopped to drink the resin from the nodules on the bole of the balsam fir trees. He made a sharp knife slice at the base of the nodule so that the sticky liquid would run down over the blade of the knife where he would collect it in his mouth. It was sweet and not unpleasant. The substance prevented scurvy, a disease often associated with sailors on long trips without fruits and vegetables. He passed the idea back down the line of men.

October passed into November, and the physical condition of the men was slowly deteriorating. Drew knew that the Chaudiere Pond and River contained a variety of fish, suggesting that the column stop to let the men fill their stomachs with fish. The nights were getting colder. So far they were lucky that the heavy snows had not arrived. Once they reached Sartigan, the local French farmers provided fresh food for the beleaguered expedition and offered some shelter from the cold. Hope was renewed that the Canadians would join them in fighting the British. Arnold knew that it was false hope and ordered even more diligence as the column approached Quebec.

Sartigan had brought back rich memories to Drew. The cabin and grave of Amelia's friend was as he had remembered them. That night, tears of remembrance froze on his whiskered cheeks.

Arnold sent couriers into Quebec to scout the situation and to set up locations to feed and house the men. Winter conditions in Canada demanded shelter and nutrition, or they would perish. It was at this point that Drew's services became unnecessary. He spoke to Colonel Arnold that he was joining Daniel Morgan's company of Virginians.

"You've been a good man, Drew LeClair. You've made a very difficult journey a little easier, thank you. Your father taught you well. Your steady hand and rifled carbine have supplied the column with desperately needed food. Morgan told me about your wish to join him. You'll be a proud member of the best company and company commander in the Continental Army."

"Thanks for the support, Sir."

The moment Drew was relieved of his responsibility to lead the expedition to Quebec, he joined Morgan's hardened frontiersmen. They had a tendency to be unruly and to oppose authority, but they faithfully followed Morgan's every whim.

The formation that reached Sartigan changed from a column of survivors to an army prepared to assault the walled city of Quebec. Yet, much had to be coordinated before specific orders could be issued. Arnold knew some people in the city and had sent them messages. Some were discovered by the authorities. He had not heard from Montgomery and was forced to wait until his formation arrived. Arnold had moved six hundred miles from Boston to Quebec with great difficulty and loss. Now he was facing a dangerous period with winter on its way and fewer men than he had planned.

In the meantime, the men and their officers purchased food and shelter from the Canadians. They were helpful, but they charged high prices. The advance element including Morgan's company with Drew as a participant crossed the St. Lawrence River at night to observe their opponents. They found a flour mill well-stocked with flour and baking facilities for bread. It was a life-saving treasure for the expedition.

Two weeks after arriving at Sartigan, Arnold moved his six hundred able-bodied men across the river to set up a camp south of the city near the Plains of Abraham where the final battle of the French and Indian War was fought. There he would wait until Montgomery arrived to supplement their manpower and supplies. Then they could mount a joint attack. He sent out people to learn about the strengths and weaknesses of the British army within the walled city proper.

Montgomery arrived with only three hundred men, but they brought with them captured supplies from Montreal of winter clothing. He also carried with him additional ammunition and some light artillery pieces which gave heart to the weary Arnold force. Terms of enlistment were up, and some men returned home. Both leaders agreed that their attack on the city should be made during a snow storm with December 31st as a target date. The men were wearing all types of clothing, so the two generals ordered that every man should wear hemlock garlands on their headgear.

During the predawn hours of December 31st a howling gale struck the area. The men circled the city, breaching the palisades and entered the lower town adjacent to the river. They could tackle the main portion of Quebec by climbing the cliffs of the walled city.

Drew was with Morgan's company when the order to attack came. He rushed down a small dark alley in the lower town when gunfire erupted from all sections of the targeted city.

# Chapter Nineteen

The night selected for an attack on Quebec was one Drew would always remember. It was his baptism into combat. He was not a soldier and was not trained to be one. Consequently, he listened carefully to everything Captain Morgan had to say or suggest to his men. He did, however, bring to the battlefield a rigid determination to do his best. He was proud to be a part of the elite group that constituted Colonel Arnold's army.

Just after dawn a raging snowstorm shrouded the city, limiting visibility to a few feet. The narrow streets of the older lower town section were abandoned. The group Drew was with ended up in a large courtyard where the Canadians and British sailors were waiting for them. They immediately fired two rapid volleys into the company of frontiersmen killing several and wounding many. Drew saw the fire belching from the barrels of the muskets and placed a random shot into the cluster of enemy troops. He quickly kneeled to reload and took careful aim at a sailor who was loading a small cannon behind a low wall. The man dropped to the ground. It was his first kill. He didn't have time to think about the incident.

Kneeling again, he began to reload his carbine. The act saved him from being captured. Captain Morgan surrendered his company after that initial volley. The enemy had an overwhelming larger number of men, to resist would be suicide and Morgan regrettably ordered his men to submit. Drew had dropped behind a large brick chimney at the outlet of the alley where the snow was swirling around him. No one took notice of him, so he crawled back out of the alley along the building's foundation until he met more of Arnold's men pulling away from the lower town.

Amid much confusion, the Patriots found the Canadians well prepared in fortified locations to repel them. The loss of men was horrific. Drew heard that General Montgomery was killed at the beginning of the assault by grapeshot. Also, Arnold had been wounded in the left leg. The situation looked hopeless to him. They had successfully surrounded the city but they lacked siege cannons and men. The British and Canadians had captured four hundred of the attacking Patriots.

Those who survived the disaster returned to the camp they had established south of the city where they looked after the wounded. Even in the face of a resounding defeat, Arnold was determined to maintain the siege. At that time, he was not aware of the large number of men that had been captured. He expected some reinforcements from Montreal, so they waited for weeks as the winter weather sapped them of strength and hope for a victorious end of the campaign.

By early May, the British Royal Navy began to arrive at Quebec with men and supplies to break the siege and to commence a campaign down the St. Lawrence to Lake Champlain, and then to the Hudson Valley. Such a strong force would separate the colonies so that they could be defeated one at a time. Arnold's leg wound healed by the time the British ships began to unload their men and supplies. He saw that further action was futile and loaded up the balance of the men and headed south on the St. Lawrence to Three Rivers. Arnold was the last man to leave Quebec. They left a large supply of military stores behind.

The retreat was quickly executed and accomplished without loss of life. Drew had saved his canoe and leaped in it to follow the retreating mass of men down the river. It was a sad time for him and the rest of the men. They had failed to take Quebec and to bring the Canadians into the fight against the British. However, their epic journey over uncharted wilderness was a testimony to the courage and determination that future generations would read about and ask: "How did they do it?"

Drew's escape from Quebec was a desperate moment. Close on their heels, British Red Coats followed in rapid pursuit. The spring thaw had opened up the rivers and melted the ice. They had passed Three Rivers and desperately paddled for the next town called Sorel at the junction of the St. Lawrence and the Richelieu River.

Ten thousand men were staging at Quebec under the command of British General John Burgoyne. Some of the troops were German dragoons from Hess. Just thinking of that powerful, well-equipped force made Drew doubt if they could defeat it on the battlefield. Burgoyne proposed using the very same route Arnold's men had taken when they fled Quebec.

Arnold knew that General John Sullivan of New Hampshire had been dispatched north by Washington to reinforce the beleaguered retreating Arnold expedition, and to secure, and hold open, a safe corridor down the Richelieu River to Fort Ticonderoga and Fort Frederick at Crown Point. The two columns met at the juncture of the two rivers. A brigade of soldiers under the command of Colonel John Stark had fought their way to the St. Lawrence, establishing a safe haven for the weary volunteers from Arnold's regiment.

Colonel John Stark was known for his courage and military skills. Drew recalled that his father had spoken about him when Stark was a ranger officer in the previous war. Drew ran his battered rawhide canoe aground near where Stark was watching for some sign of the approaching British troops and was waiting for them. The canoe collapsed in pieces on some unseen rapids. Drew grabbed his carbine and leaped from the foundering little canoe. Luckily he had taken the precaution of keeping his pack strapped to his shoulders.

Stark saw his predicament and waded into the stream to assist Drew. "You did well to keep your powder dry, son. The enemy is close behind you. Keep moving down the riverbank. I have a group of boats ready to leave on short notice," he pointed downstream. "You can ride down with me. How many are behind you, son?"

"I was the rear guard, Sir. Colonel Arnold is going on to Montreal to check on that situation," Drew told him, wading out of the water.

Stark's deep eyes and bushy eyebrows softened as he evaluated this stranger. "For a moment I thought you were one of the Penacooks that accompanied Colonel Arnold up the Kennebec," Stark said.

"No, Sir, my mother is a Penacook, but my father is a French marine veteran of the Indian wars. I was Arnold's pathfinder up the Kennebec. My family runs a tavern and ferry on the Kennebec."

"You've been away from home for a long time, son. Come, we should get out of here. I spotted one of Burgoyne's scouts around the curve in the river," he said, running towards the last boat tied up beside the river. "You take the bow, son, and I'll row. Give that paddle all you've got. We'll soon draw musket fire from the British vanguard. What's your name?"

"I'm Drew LeClair, Sir. I believe we have mutual friends in Portsmouth. My mother and a Mrs. Lavina Cullen are best friends.

Stark dipped his paddle deep into the clear water with powerful arms propelling the boat over the water as fast as a slim canoe. "Daniel and his lovely wife, Lavina, have been dear friends for many years. When was the last time you heard from home, Drew?"

"Nothing since I left in September of last year. Would it be possible to write to them, Sir?"

"I'll see that any letters you may write are sent out in my dispatch pouch," Stark announced. "Mails still move about the colonies with a minimum of interruption. We can thank Ben Franklin for establishing a very efficient posting system several years ago."

"Where are we headed now, Colonel Stark?" Drew asked, wondering what he was going to do. "I signed on with Colonel Arnold to blaze a trail through the wilderness to Quebec. A large number of the men have already gone home."

"And what do you want to do, Drew LeClair?" Stark took a liking to this sturdy, plain-speaking young man.

It was a pointed question Drew had been asking himself ever since he left Quebec. "I have a son back home on the Kennebec. I'd like him to grow up in a country that respects the rights of its people instead of a distant Parliament who looks upon us as workers who owe their existence to the Crown. We are not a religious family like some, but we do believe in the

151

rights our God gave us to be free men. I'd like to join your New Hampshire regiment until the first of the year when the armies traditionally go into winter quarters. I'm a good shot with my rifled carbine."

"I've been admiring that fine weapon you carry," Colonel Stark smiled. "I'll be proud to enroll you into our New Hampshire regiment. It makes up half of the brigade I command. We're heading to Fort Ticonderoga and Crown Point on the southern portion of the lake. It appears as if the British intend to divide the colonies by driving down the Hudson Valley to New York. That means that we'll be the main source of resistance when they arrive. Our task is to stop their advance south. If we are successful, it may end the war soon. If we fail, our chances are in the hands of our God. It promises to be a troubled area, Drew LeClair."

Drew understood the significance of Stark's sobering statement. Colonel Arnold had mentioned the same thing. "I'll be proud to serve under your command, Colonel Stark."

"For now, I'll place you on my staff as a courier."

"That sounds good to me. I'm anxious to get off a letter to my family. I've been keeping a journal of events ever since I left home on the Kennebec," Drew declared, looking upstream.

"You'll be a valuable addition to my staff, Son. Now paddle as hard as you can, the enemy is right on our tail and is within musket range," Stark exclaimed, burying his paddle deep in the water.

Remnants of Arnold's defeated force escaped down the St. Lawrence River to the Richelieu River and then into Lake Champlain. As the retreating columns approached Crown Point and Fort Ticonderoga they were temporarily free of the threatening Burgoyne forces which went into a staging posture at the northern end of the lake. Colonel Arnold had been promoted to Brigadier General and proceeded to Skenesborough where he intended to build boats and floats to oppose the British presence on the lake.

Stark's brigade was ordered to build fortifications and facilities for troops at Chimney Point across the lake from Fort Ticonderoga. The view from the top was breathtaking. The men spent weeks building barracks and constructing cannon emplacements on top of the prominent height. The first day Drew arrived at Chimney Point, he wrote a letter to his family describing events on his long journey to Lake Champlain. Stark had promised him that it would go out in his next dispatch packet which passed almost on a daily basis between his command and New Hampshire. The first letter from home arrived as he was shoveling earth for a gun redoubt.

Colonel Stark personally handed him the letter. "You have mail, Drew. You're a good worker. I'm glad you joined us. Take a break and enjoy some news from home. I'm going to do the same thing."

Drew wiped the sweat from his brow and accepted the letter. Sitting on a stump he anxiously read:

June 20, 1776

My dear Son,

You'll never know how worried we have been about your safety. Our prayers were answered when Captain Jones arrived to give us your letter. You've been through a lot, and we are so proud of your service to our noble cause.

Your son, Abel, Jr., is doing fine and growing like a weed. He's a lot like his father, curious and caring. He helps a lot around the tavern. Ana has been wonderful with him. We would have had a hard time if she had not come to work with us. She's become like a member of the family. Her uncle stops by whenever he can. He's been successful in capturing several British merchant ships filled with supplies. He delivers them to Newport, Rhode Island, or to Boston. He's a true patriot and I'm proud to call him a friend.

We knew that the effort to take Quebec had failed. When news of the event arrived, we could only imagine the worst for you. Those few who returned back down the Kennebec informed us of your progress. It was a valiant attempt to bring the Canadians into the war as an ally. I was not surprised they refused.

Your new commanding officer, Colonel John Stark, is one of the best soldiers in the Continental Army. I remember him from the dark days of the French and Indian War on the harsh frontier. His deeds of daring and courage were known throughout the region. He was always a foe to those who threatened liberty and freedom. His respect for the Native Americans was sincere. He championed their cause when it was not popular. You are fortunate to be serving with his brigade.

Be assured that we are doing just fine, Son. You probably have not heard about our experience with our neighbors from Falmouth. While you were guiding the expedition to Canada, several British warships anchored in Casco Bay and fired hot shells into the city, forcing the residents to flee for their safety. A few were killed in the bombardment. Many suffered terribly in the cold months of winter trying to get to shelter here on the Kennebec or south toward Portsmouth, New Hampshire.

We all send you our love and prayers, dear Son.

Dad and the gang at the tavern.

P.S. I forgot to mention that Pru's husband was killed at sea where he joined the Royal Navy to fight against the patriots. Pru was saddened by the news, but she was also relieved of his reign of terror. He turned out to be a bad choice for her. She's doing just fine now at the trading post.

The day after Drew received the letter, Colonel Stark called for an officer's conference. Something big had taken place! Shortly after, he called the regiment on top of the hill to gather for an announcement. The men lined up by companies. Drew was selected to participate in firing a ceremonial volley. When the men were assembled, Stark climbed up on a gun carriage to address the group. A soft prevailing westerly wind swept the hilltop. Stark's deep-set eyes and bushy eyebrows gave him a stern appearance, but those who knew him were comforted by his firm stand as a patriot and a foe against tyranny.

"Men," he announced in an authoritative voice that carried throughout the assembly area. "I've called you together to celebrate a joyous occasion. I have here in my hands a copy of a document that has been issued by the Continental Congress. It puts into words the ideals that describe our case against British rule. It is called the Declaration of Independence. The beautiful words give our cause a righteous nobility. Rest easy, men, I want to read portions of the document to you. This is a day you can celebrate with your children and grandchildren. I quote:

> *When in the course of human events, it becomes necessary for one people to dissolve the political bonds which have connected them with another, and to assume, among the powers of the earth, the separate and equal station to which the laws of nature and of nature's God entitle them, a decent respect to the opinions of mankind requires that they should declare the causes which impel them to separate.*

> *We hold these truths to be self-evident: That all men are created equal; that they are endowed by their Creator with certain unalienable rights; among these are life, liberty, and the pursuit of happiness; that, to secure these rights, governments are instituted among men, deriving their just powers from the consent of the governed; that whenever any form of government becomes destructive of these ends, it is the right of the people to alter or abolish it, and to institute new government, laying its foundation on such principles, and organizing its powers in such form as to them shall seem most likely to affect their safety and happiness...*

> *We, therefore, the representatives of the United States of America, in General Congress assembled, appealing to the Supreme Judge of the world for the rectitude of our intentions, do, in the name and by the authority of the good people of these colonies, solemnly publish and declare, that these United Colonies are, and of right ought to be, FREE AND INDEPENCENT STATES,... we mutually pledge to each other our lives, our fortunes, and our sacred honor."*

When Stark completed the reading of the document he called for the honorary color guard to fire a thirteen gun salute to the newly established United States of America. A young lieutenant solemnly ordered the guard front and center, giving loud and precise orders to load, prime, cock and fire. All thirteen muskets went off as one. Loud cheers and whistles erupted from the regiment. It was a historical time that made Drew proud to be a part of the fight for freedom and to be an American. Later that night he wrote a letter home:

July 7, 1776

Dear Folks,

Today we celebrated our Declaration of Independence by officially calling the mountain we have been fortifying Independence Mountain. It was a day that made all of our hardships worthwhile.

This is a beautiful section of our new country. I'm sitting in my tent looking over Fort Ticonderoga on the west shore of Lake Champlain. It's a peaceful scene that reminds me of home.

I was saddened to learn about Pru's husband. I always knew he had Tory leanings. He seemed to enjoy confrontations. I think often about the times Pru and I spent together as young children. Over the years she was my best friend. When I left for Arnold's expedition she was almost overwhelmed. Her father was of little help to her at the trading post. I hope that situation has changed. I'm enclosing a separate note for her in this dispatch to you. Please pass it on to her.

It's plain to see the strategy the British intend to use against us. I saw some of the troops landing at Quebec. Burgoyne's army is a potent force, well trained, well equipped, and looking for a fight. Colonel Stark is hopeful that we can stop them here at the southern end of Lake Champlain. We pray that it is so!

Our troops are probably more motivated than the British, but they are woefully lacking in supplies and equipment of every type. The men have not been paid one cent since the fighting began. I'd follow Colonel John Stark to the gates of hell if he ordered us to do so. He inspires the men to do their best by looking after their welfare. I feel privileged to be a part of his regiment from New Hampshire.

The sun is setting behind the mountains to the west, casting orange shadows on the water below. I have no candles for my lantern, so I bid you all goodnight. I miss all of you very much.

Love,

Drew

# Chapter Twenty

The war was not going well for the Patriots. The English had taken control of Long Island and New York City and several forts on the southern portion of the Hudson River Valley in preparation of their plans to drive north to meet Burgoyne's force. There was also a large British force making a wide flanking movement from Fort Niagara to Lake Erie and the Mohawk River with plans to meet at the juncture of the Hudson River at Albany. The Royal Navy controlled all of the Atlantic. The future looked grim. Hope was a precious and scarce commodity dwindling fast.

Stark's regiment was building a formidable bastion of defense on Mount Independence. Benedict Arnold had been very industrious at Skenesboro building floats, gondolas, and small ships to use against the British at the northern end of the lake. He eventually sailed against them in a valiant attempt to slow their progress and lessen their ability to conduct a successful campaign. His efforts caused Burgoyne to go into winter quarters. Arnold's small navy was totally destroyed, but he had stalled the invasion, buying precious time for the Continental Army to secure a victory somewhere, no matter how small. Morale within the troops was at its lowest point possible.

General Washington ordered Sullivan's Division to move south two hundred miles. Stark was given command of a brigade which included the New Hampshire regiment Drew had joined. They made the move to meet Washington at Newton, Pennsylvania, in record time. Washington had planned a daring attack across the partially frozen Delaware

River at the winter quarters of a large number of Hessian troops. Success depended on surprise. Stark was given the task of being the spearhead of the attacking force. Once the army had crossed the river, Stark's brigade was to follow along the eastern shore into Trenton, New Jersey where the German troops were celebrating Christmas in large, comfortable homes.

Stark led his brigade into the heart of the British encampments dealing death and destruction along the way. Their surprise was complete. The Hessians were unable to put up a meaningful defense. Stark personally pounded on the doors of several houses filled with enemy troops, demanding their surrender. Drew was at his side, astonished at the tenacity and speed that carried the Americans into the British stronghold. Within two hours the town had been captured. British losses were heavy, and many were taken prisoner. The Americans never lost a man! The victory lifted morale several degrees.

The success at Trenton led to another battle at nearby Princeton, New Jersey. Washington had seen an opportunity to push the British out of New Jersey, and he was successful in doing so for the time being. Drew accompanied Stark who was his normal self at the head of his brigade into the environs of Princeton. The defeat of the large detachments there gave the Americans large quantities of military stores that were desperately needed.

Prior to the battles for New Jersey, the Continental Army was shrinking by alarming numbers from desertion and from the expiration of enlistments at the end of the year. Stark had called his brigade together and had asked for the men to serve for another six weeks. He promised them that if the Congress could not make the payments, he would sell off some of his property to do so. Every man in the brigade reenlisted until they went into winter quarters. Drew was proud to be part of such a dedicated brigade.

Colonel Stark had proven his competence and dedication to the cause by his actions in combat. When the list of promotions from Congress arrived, his name was not on the list for promotion to Brigadier General even though he had been commanding a brigade for the past year with distinction.

Washington's army marched into Morristown where they planned to stay for the winter. Drew accompanied Stark and several hundred men back to New Hampshire anxious to be with their families for the balance of the winter months. They arrived at Derryfield, cold, hungry, and physically worn out. A ferry took them across the Merrimack River close to Stark's home.

Stark stepped ashore and turned to Drew. "You've been a fine trooper, Drew LeClair. Your father taught you well. There's a freight convoy heading for Portsmouth. Catch a lift on it and rest your tired legs. Try to get a lift out of Portsmouth to the Kennebec. That's a busy harbor. Good luck, son."

"Thank you, Sir. It was a privilege to serve under your command. I'm excited to be on my way home," Drew replied, shaking his gnarled hand. He then hopped on board a freight wagon filled with firewood destined for Portsmouth.

A week later, Drew was dropped off at the family dock during a severe northeastern storm that buffeted the water, limiting visibility. The schooner was one of many privateers that were the main source of supplies for the Continental Army. Drew looked around, choked with emotion. He never thought he would see this place again. Drew slipped his pack on his back and cradled his carbine in one arm as he waved to the schooner captain and leaped onto the family dock.

The steep climb up the steps from the landing in the swirling wind took his breath away, stopped to look around. Two feet of snow blanketed the area. No one was outside. Nothing had really changed. The ferry was anchored for the night on the west bank of the river. Smoke curled from the two chimneys of the house and tavern. He smiled, remembering how much effort it took to maintain the fireplaces in the two structures. He had been away for seventeen months, almost a year and a half. His rough appearance was frightening. He had lost about twenty-five pounds, and the clothes he wore were tattered and torn. Two different boots covered his cold feet that were also wrapped in two blankets. Matched pairs of footwear were scarce in the Army.

He was cold and chilled to the bone as he made his way into the main entrance of the tavern. The warmth of the room was welcome. Two customers were eating at a table close to the fireplace. He did not recognize them and removed his pack and leaned his carbine against the wall next to the hearth. Then he backed up to the heat, absorbing as much as possible. Drew had been cold most of the time since he left home.

Ben entered the room with an armful of wood and dumped it in the wood box next to Drew. "A fire does feel good on a night such as this, doesn't it, Sir?"

Drew smiled at the gentle Penacook. "You don't recognize me, do you, Ben?"

Ben came closer to look into his eyes, "My God, it's you, Drew," he exclaimed, grasping him in a bear hug. "Welcome home, welcome home... we've been so worried for you!"

Drew returned his embrace. It was nice to be back where he belonged. "How are Mother and Father and little Abel?"

"Your parents are doing just fine. Having you home safe will be the answer to their prayers. Abel, Jr., is the center of attention in this place. Your mother is teaching him to read and write. Your folks have been wonderful to me. I love them as if they were my own. Your son is growing up in a household filled with love. Now, let me get you something hot to drink and something to eat. I have some kedgeree still warm."

"That would be most welcome, Ben. Thank you."

Drew pulled a chair closer to the fireside and removed his boots, or what was left of them. For the past month he had woven a blanket around each foot to keep them from freezing. Suddenly, without warning, his parents ran through the shed to the dining room. His mother was speechless as she collected him in her arms and held him close to her heart. Tears of relief and thanksgiving ran freely down her bronze cheeks.

She turned him towards the flickering flames so that she could get a good look at him. She gasped at the dark deep-set of his eyes and the penetrating stare that looked but did not see. "My Son, what have they done to you?" she cried, holding him again.

"It's been a long journey, Mother. I'll be alright," he explained, burying his face in her coal-black hair.

Abel quietly stood beside the pair. His son had seen too much of war. He understood that and knew that time will heal the wounds be they physical or emotional. Abel, too, had experienced the same thing. The load had been almost unbearable for him until he met the love of his life. Their son was a lot like his mother. The quiet, sensitive type always carried the scars of war for a long, long time. He knew… he knew…!

Abel emotionally hugged his son and Marie. "Your son is sleeping soundly at the house in your old room. He is a lot like his father and has been worried like the rest of us for your safe return."

"It's so good to be home," Drew cried. He loved these two people more than life. "Would it be asking too much if I had a warm bath? I've dreamed of that for the past month. These clothes and the remnants from the boots can all be burned," he explained in a wavering voice. "But for now, I need hot food and tea. Ben is getting some for me. I've been hungry and cold every day since I left home a year and a half ago."

"We understand, Son," Abel guided him to a chair close to the fireplace. "I know how it is when you've been chilled to the bone. A cold body can absorb a lot of heat."

"I'm going back to the house to get you a clean change of clothes, Drew," Marie told them. "Ah, these old things should definitely be burned. If you want, I'll give you a haircut and your father can shave off your beard. It's probably the home of a few insects."

"I think you're right, Mother," he smiled, shaking his head.

Marie and Abel acknowledged the smile with another hug. That little boy part of their son was still present. They had much to be thankful for. The new year of 1777 was starting on a positive note for the LeClair family.

After eating his fill and consuming two mugs of steaming tea, Drew washed layers of grime from his body in the warm water that had been placed in an empty room in the tavern where Ben had a fireplace burning. Fresh underclothes and a warm nightgown on top of a full stomach induced him into an exhaustive sleep that lasted for twenty-four hours. The storm outside shrieked and howled about the tavern shifting light snow into every nook and cranny. It was not a good night to be outside exposed to the fury of Nature.

Drew opened his eyes, surprised that it was still dark. The storm outside had abated some, blanketing the area with a few inches of fresh snow. The flickering flames from the fireplace cast shadows about the walls and ceiling. For a moment he did not know where he was. A beard had been a part of him ever since the Kennebec expedition. Now that his father had shaved it off his skin itched. It was then that he knew he was home. His mother had little patience for bearded faces. He smiled seeing the pile of clean clothes on a table beside the fireplace. He climbed out of bed and dressed thinking how nice it was to get dressed in a warm room for a change.

Ben quietly entered the room with an armful of firewood. "I hope I didn't disturb you, Drew. It's cold outside, and the fires have kept me busy. You slept well."

"Thanks, Ben. Sleeping in a warm room is one luxury I haven't had in months," Drew smiled at the faithful young Penacook. "You know, Ben, as time goes by you look more and more like your sister, Amelia. A day never passed that she was not in my thoughts."

"I'm sure that my dear sister still guides our steps, Drew. Surely her love never ceased when she was called to Heaven," Ben replied.

"Your faith is still strong, Ben. I envy you for that. Sometimes on the trail when things were bleak, I was able to find comfort and direction from the memories of the times we shared together. What time is it, Ben?"

"You've slept for twenty-four hours, Drew. It's now about eight o'clock in the evening. We only have two quests. The weather has stalled traveling. Ana and Little Abel are downstairs anxious to see you."

"Well," he exclaimed with a grin, "it's time I stopped being so lazy."

"I'll prepare some oatmeal and tea for you, Drew. It's nice to have you home."

"It's nice to be home, Ben. Thanks for keeping the home fires burning. I remember how much work it takes in the cold months. I'll be down shortly."

Six year old Abel, Jr., was sitting in a chair with a pillow under him eating an apple pie with a glass of milk when Drew entered the dining room. He looked up at his father, dropped out of his chair, and ran into his open arms. Holding his son after all the long months of separation brought tears to Drew's eyes.

"Don't cry, Daddy," he said, looking into his eyes. Even at that young age, Little Abel could see changes from the man that had left him a year and a half ago.

"It's only because I'm happy to see you again, Abel," he replied, holding his son to look at him. Abel, Jr., was a handsome little boy with crisp dark eyes, black hair and pronounced cheek bones that reflected his heritage. "You've grown a lot since we last met. You have your mother's eyes and mouth. Everyone tells me that you are a very good helper here at the tavern."

"Grandfather has told us all about the places you have been far, far from home. I was afraid you'd get lost and not be able to find your way back home."

Ana entered the room and rushed to Drew. "Your homecoming has brightened this family, Drew. We've been worried for you," she embraced him and kissed him on the cheek. "My uncle has been diligent in keeping us informed of events you participated in and of your arduous journey out of Canada to Fort Ticonderoga."

"You're looking good, Ana. Mother told me that you were at Pru's place when I arrived. How is she doing, and how is Pearl?" he asked, concerned about his friend of many years.

"Both are doing well, Drew. She'll be so glad that you've come home. Her husband was a burden for her. The day he left, he got drunk and smashed up some of the trading post in one of his raging tantrums. His parting farewell was a cruel blow to her cheek that became swollen and took a long time to heal. His passing is an act from a merciful God."

"I'm sure it is, Ana," Drew replied, contemplating what she had said. "Say, do you have any more apple pies like Abel is eating?"

Ana smiled at him. "Your mother never lets us run out of our trademark dish, Drew," Ana exclaimed, running into the kitchen.

# Chapter Twenty-One

After everyone had gone to bed, Drew and his father sat beside the fireplace in the tavern discussing the war. Abel had often talked about the situation with his long-time friend, John Boisvert. As time passed after the death of John's wife, John was becoming more and more disconnected from the events around him. Whether it was senile dysfunction or loss of the ability to cope with everyday problems, Abel was never certain about his friend. It was a sad fact because he had always looked up to John for advice. However, Abel was probably as well informed about unfolding events as anyone in the area. The ships that sailed and stopped on the Kennebec from distant ports were a rich source of current information about the war and other current events. Newspapers from the eastern seaboard were delivered on a weekly basis.

"The country is encouraged by Washington's brilliant success at Trenton and Princeton. How does the average soldier rate General Washington, son?"

Drew took a long sip from his tea mug, staring into the red coals of the fire. It was always a focal point that helped to sort out a person's thoughts. "I know that Colonel Stark liked Washington's boldness in those two battles. Yet, he was critical of the long string of losses that was destroying the morale of the Continental Army since Bunker Hill. I have a feeling that Colonel Arnold would pick a time and place to confront the British forces in a battle that would determine the winner or loser."

"I expect you're right about Arnold. He certainly is a determined and aggressive officer," Abel agreed. "Earlier on I thought that Washington was unsure about himself and his Army and avoided a showdown pitched battle. My old friend in Portsmouth, Daniel Cullen, an avid student of tactics and strategy, gives Washington high praise for not wasting the Army in battles it cannot win. In every engagement, he has successfully disengaged his forces, still intact to fight, when conditions favor the Continental Army. Hit and run tactics do help to wear down the enemy. Washington has shown himself an agile and decisive leader in saving the Army to fight only on his terms. Trenton and Princeton are perfect examples."

"I hadn't thought about it that way," Drew admitted. "Washington is certainly a magnificent sight on horseback. He led the main flanking charge at Trenton with outstanding courage and dash. Colonel Stark thinks the war will be won or lost when Burgoyne's forces reach the lower portion of Lake Champlain at Fort Ticonderoga. If he cannot be stopped before he reaches the lower Hudson Valley, the British have the opportunity to defeat us piecemeal with the help of their powerful Royal Navy."

"It looks like Stark is correct. He's a seasoned campaigner and a masterful leader of men in combat." Abel yawned and got up to bank the fire for the night. "I'm ready to turn in, son. It's nice to have you home with us. You need to recuperate from the rigors of heavy campaigning. I speak from experience. Eat and rest to your heart's content, son. Goodnight."

"Goodnight, Father. Is John able to run the Boisvert Trading Post?"

"He helps some, but Pru handles all transactions and has done a good job. She asks for you every time I see her."

"Tomorrow I'm going over for a visit. That warm bed upstairs will feel good tonight. I'll see you in the morning, Father."

The next morning, Drew got up long after sunrise and went to the tavern to eat breakfast with his mother and Abel, Jr.

"Your father told me that you planned to see Pru today," said his mother, eating one of the apple pies she had proudly introduced to the area.

"I never understood how she got involved with Joseph Mason. He was nothing but a braggart and a low-down cheat."

Marie nodded her head to acknowledge her son's description of Pru's dead husband.

"Pru changed after the death of her mother. They were extremely close. I still mourn my dear friend Rosalee. Poor John, he lost the will to fight and simply gave up. Pru takes good care of him. She's increased business at the trading post so that they are much more comfortable than ever economically."

"The Captain of the ship that dropped me off said that traffic on the river has been quite brisk lately. He told me that some of the Tories that have been displaced in Rhode Island and Massachusetts were settling in Maine. Is that the case on the Kennebec?"

"I've heard that some have quietly taken up residence," his mother replied.

"Some of the toughest skirmishes I experienced involved colonists who have taken up arms with the British," he informed her.

"I don't defend them, son. Most of the Colonists never relinquished their ties to England. They simply refused to be treated like second rate citizens by the mother country. Washington was not in favor of a complete disconnect from England in the beginning of the conflict. We simply refused to be treated like slaves by an uncaring Parliament. Your roots are with France and the original Americans. I'm more concerned with their just place in our society than I am with dislocated Tories. However, the war is not over, and we must defeat the most powerful Army and Navy in the world before anyone's destiny is determined."

Drew listened to his mother and got up to kiss her on the forehead. "My father chose well. You've always made me proud of who and what I am."

She embraced him and checked to see if Abel, Jr. was finished with his oatmeal. "These long winter days are good for educating our younger generation," she smiled and kissed him on the cheek. "Your son is the kind of pupil a teacher likes. He's alert and quick to grasp things. A good mind should never be wasted. The good Reverend at Memphramagog had the gift of cultivating a curious mind."

"The Reverend had an apt student in you, Mother."

"Well, come, Junior, we have work to do. Several of the students close by come to our morning sessions."

Drew laughed and hugged Junior. "Enjoy the day with Grandmother, son. I'm going to visit Pru and your friend Pearl this morning. Thanks for everything, Mother." He watched two of the most important people in his life walk out the door hand in hand. The sight warmed his heart.

The path along the west bank of the Kennebec River between the tavern and the Boisvert Trading Post was well-worn in the summertime. This winter it was filled with windswept snow several inches thick and in places frozen bare ground. Salt air from the tidal water had a tendency to melt some of the snow so that it did not reach the heavy snow cap of the inland portions of Maine. The river was at high tide with the water close to overflowing of the banks. The river had always fascinated Drew. It was the economic lifeline to the communities settled along its banks. Large ocean going vessels were capable, when controlled by experienced pilots, to travel up to the Gardiner rapids, just south of Augusta. The first merchant ship to successfully travel up to Gardiner took place while Benedict Arnold was supplying the Quebec expedition. It was piloted by the skilled sailor, James LaBree, when he was sixteen years old.

Drew had been thinking about how Captain Jones took his shallow draft schooner all the way to Augusta. Few patriots had as much fire in the belly for the cause of freedom as the courageous Captain Jones. Drew smiled; he had thoroughly enjoyed his sea trips with the intrepid sailor. He intended to speak to the Captain about the possibility of him purchasing a merchant ship to trade up and down the Atlantic coast once the war was over. He was listless and uncertain what he wanted to do with the rest of his life. Before he left Colonel Stark, Drew had told him that he would be glad to serve under his command at any time.

He recalled his exact words: "The politicians may lose this war for the soldiers, Drew LeClair. Mark my words, this country will win or lose the contest in the Hudson Valley much the way the war with France was won. If Burgoyne is able to link up with British troops from the west and from the south, we cannot assemble a strong enough army to defeat them. Engagements in the Carolinas and Virginia are important, but the road to ultimate victory lies within the Champlain-Hudson Valley corridor. Washington is aware of that and is frantically concentrating forces to stop the invader at that crucial passage to the heart of our colonial empire."

Whenever he or his father looked at a map of the region, they, too, agreed with the seasoned campaigner. It was close enough for them to have cause for concern!

By the time Drew could see the smoke curling from the Boisvert's chimneys he was thoroughly chilled. There was always a brisk breeze that followed the river basin. He noticed that Pru and her father, John, had enlarged the storage capacity of the original house. It extended close to the loading dock on the river making it more efficient to store the goods and supplies. Drew could smell the sweet aroma of bacon and hams being smoked in the smokehouse at the rear of the house. It reminded him of his father's own smokehouse. Every homestead had one. Even months after a batch of ham and bacon had been cured, the tantalizing aroma remained.

A small schooner was tied up to the dock. Drew recognized it as being one belonging to Mudge Jackson's warehouse at the mouth of the Kennebec River. Two workers were unloading supplies onto the dock. The lower portions of the river never froze, so the boats freely traveled that portion all year round. Drew waved to the workers as he stepped onto the large porch entrance to the trading post.

Upon letting himself in, he was surprised at how neat and clean the well-stocked shelves were. John and Pru had worked hard to build the reputation they now enjoyed of fair dealings and prices for sound values. He looked around the interior and saw Pearl sitting at a table next to the fireplace eating a bowl of oatmeal. She looked up and stared at him for a long time.

"You don't remember me, do you, Pearl?"

"Are you Drew LeClair?" she asked. "Mother was just talking about you to Grandfather.

"Yes, I'm Drew LeClair. You've grown since I last saw you. My father has told me that you come to my mother's reading classes. It's nice to see you again, Pearl."

A cry of excitement echoed from the trading post storage room. "Is that voice I hear, Drew?" Pru exclaimed, running into his outstretched arms. "My dear friend has come home to us at last. I've been frightened for you, Drew." She laid her head against his chest and wept for joy.

Warm memories from the past with Pru ran through his consciousness. She had always been steadfast to their friendship. She released him and wiped her eyes to see him better. His deep-set eyes reflected the horrors he had experienced. "We'll have to erase those ugly images, dear friend. Your folks kept me informed when they heard from you. Our prayers have been answered. My most precious memories have always involved you. When I was rough and abrupt and spontaneous, you remained calm and gentle and faithful to our friendship. Those memories have sustained me for a long time. Do you ever think of Acadia, Drew?"

He smiled, enjoying her enthusiasm. "I remember, Pru. How could I ever forget? Sometimes you shocked me. I was a little shy back then."

"Father is still resting. He was up late packing away supplies. Please take off your coat while I get you a hot tea. It's the devil's drink for us, but we still like it. I think often of our time in Acadia with Mother and Jodi," she said, pouring two tankards of steaming hot tea.

"I heard about Joseph, Pru. I'm sorry for you and Pearl. Both of you deserved better. Thanks for the tea. We still enjoy it, too. It's cold out there this morning."

Pru studied Drew beside the fireplace. That serious and gentle side of her friend was still present, but the lines about his mouth and eyes gave him a stern and severe look that was totally out of character for him. She recalled seeing those same penetrating stares in her father when she was a little girl.

"Now that you're home I hope it's for good, Drew. You've seen enough. You've done your part. I can never know what you've seen or experienced, but I know you well enough that those who care for you are anxious to erase those images from your mind."

He never knew how to answer such a comment. His mother and father said the same things. "I never appreciated what my father and yours went through in the earlier Indian and French wars. The experience is a humbling one and makes a man ask the question 'Is our cause worth the blood being shed on both sides?' I personally answered that question in the affirmative. I don't hate those who think differently from me, but I do hate those individuals in power who seek to limit my freedom and my God-given rights as a man. The injustices and tyranny that Parliament has imposed upon her brothers in the colonies are justification enough to defend our rights. I believe in my heart that we are on the correct side of that issue."

"I never heard it described so well, Drew. Father is afraid we are not strong enough to defeat the British army."

"That statement haunts all of us, Pru," Drew replied. "As for me, I plan to recuperate for the winter and help out here at home where I can. Come Spring, I will evaluate if I can make a contribution to our cause."

Pru threw another log on the fire and sat beside Drew. "I know that these unsettled times require sacrifices from all of us. I'm selfish enough to admit that I'd hate to see you face the guns again, Drew. Do you know how much you're missed when you're away?"

"I can understand your position, Pru. I like to think that we have the opportunity to create a better life for Pearl and Abel in a country that is free to seek its own destiny. That is important to me."

"Is there a place for me in your life, Drew?"

The direct question was not unlike Pru, but it gave him pause to think about his answer. "Life without my old friend is unthinkable. Just seeing you again is the answer to my hopes and dreams. You've always been a big part of my life, Pru…"

She looked away and wiped tears that welled into her eyes. "I never stopped loving you, Drew. Never…"

He stood up and took her into his arms, "Let's take things one day at a time, Pru. I can't imagine life without you. Once we have settled this conflict, it would be comforting for me to look forward to a life that we had always planned even as little children together…"

"What are you trying to say, Drew?"

He kissed her and held her close to his heart. "I've loved you from a distance for so long…"

"Will you marry me when this cursed war is over?"

"However this war turns out, yes, I'll marry you, Pru."

# Chapter Twenty-Two

News from the battlefields continued to be disheartening to the colonists. All eyes were focused on the major threat to the future prosecution of the war effort in the Champlain-Hudson corridor. General Burgoyne's plans to take Fort Ticonderoga were evident. The fort on the west bank at the southern end of the lake was the main bastion of defense for the colonists and had been reinforced by Washington as much as was humanly possible.

Early in July, the British struck with overwhelming force and captured the fort. The Continental Army garrison was able to abandon the fort with minimal losses. They retreated into western Vermont, fighting a successful delayed action strategy. The colonies were in danger of being broken into smaller parcels and defeated one at a time by the concentration of superior enemy formations. This hysteria prompted reaction from the surrounding colonies to send forces to counteract the massive English effort in the Hudson Valley.

Captain Jones pulled his schooner to the LeClair dock and secured it shortly after word had been circulated that Fort Ticonderoga had been captured. He was excited and alarmed about the news he had picked up at Portsmouth, New Hampshire. The people of Vermont were afraid that elements of Burgoyne's Army were about to invade and loot their territory, including the rich Connecticut River valley for forage, food and military supplies, especially horses for their German dragoon troops. The New Hampshire response to Vermont's plea for help rapidly produced a full militia regiment to be commanded by Brigadier General John Stark. Vermont troops were in constant retreat. Time was most important.

Drew asked Captain Jones, "When is the New Hampshire regiment going to Vermont?"

"As soon as its numbers have assembled at the old abandoned Fort Number Four site in Charlestown. The area is being used as a staging area for men and supplies. Several men here on the Kennebec have volunteered for this operation."

Drew thought about what could happen to his homeland if the worst fears became reality. "I trust General Stark. If this invasion by the British is going to be stopped, he's the man who can make it happen. I trust his instincts." Leaving home again would place an additional burden on Drew's family, and Pru would be furious with him.

Captain Jones unfurled a flag he carried in his hand. "This is the new flag that the Continental Congress voted to represent the United States of America, our new country. The thirteen stripes of alternate red and white and the thirteen stars arranged in a circle on a blue field represent a new constellation. I purchased several of them to deliver to my friends. One is flying from the mast of my schooner. This one is for your family, Drew."

"Thank you, Captain. Please sit and enjoy a hot tea that Ana is serving us now."

"Mr. LeClair just came into the tavern, Uncle," Ana announced, serving the tea. "He's anxious to hear what you have to say."

"Do you bring bad news, Captain?" Abel asked, taking a seat beside him.

Captain Jones explained the situation to Abel and pointed to the flag in Drew's hand. Abel looked at his son with inquiring eyes. The old soldier saw that empty stare that distant war drums were capable of cultivating in young men. "You've already made up your mind to go, haven't you, son?"

"Knowing that Stark will be in command gives me hope for the future. The country is at an important crisis point right now. Stark and the New Hampshire regiment of militia may be the instrument that turns the tide. If we do nothing, then the enemy has already won," Drew replied firmly.

Abel placed a hand on his son's shoulder. "If I was a younger man, I'd go with you. The British have shown us their strategy for our demise. Just perhaps their arrogance and their acceptance of a very long supply train may be their undoing. I agree with your impression of Stark. He's one of the best combat officers in the colonies. How soon are you leaving for Portsmouth, Captain?"

"Within the hour, Abel. We're working against the clock. Carriages with four teams are running shuttle from Portsmouth to Number Four filled with men and supplies."

Drew realized that he did not have time to notify Pru of his decision to leave. "Father, would you explain the situation to Pru after we've left? She'll be angry at me, but that can't be helped. Just maybe this plan to oppose the British thrust into new territory may be one step too far..."

"I like that attitude, son. Now, we've got to gather what you need in your pack. I'll speak to Pru after you've gone."

"Thanks. I'll go say good-bye to Mother, Ben, and Ana, and I better change my clothes."

Three days later, Drew jumped off a wagon of supplies at the great meadow site near the abandoned Fort Number Four. He had a full pack on his back and a woolen blanket wrapped around the pack. He was adequately supplied for the warm months of the summer. Volunteers for the militia signed on for one month duration. Drew inquired where he could find General John Stark. One of the volunteers pointed to a cluster of men close to the bank of the river.

Stark was studying the roster of volunteers and recognized Drew approaching him. "Is that you, Drew?"

"Yes, Sir. An old friend told me that you were assembling a regiment for duty in the Hudson Valley," Drew quickly replied.

Stark was not one to smile often, but Drew's presence touched him. "We can use all the good men we can get. Vermont's call for help cannot be refused." He turned to an aide sitting at a table. "This man's name is Drew LeClair. I want him on my personal staff."

Ten minutes later, Drew was at the head of a column on his way to Manchester, Vermont. He was pleased to have his old job as courier to the general. The officer in charge of the column was a Lieutenant John Holmes from Amherst, New Hampshire. He told Drew that Stark had been sending troops in small parcels to their destination as soon as they were organized and sworn in. As soon as the full complement was concentrated he planned to lead them into action. He had already sent out several scouts to gather any intelligence available on the detached units from General Burgoyne's Army. Drew's function was to act as a messenger for the battalions within the regiment. It was imperative that all units received the same information as soon as possible in order for them to act in unison.

Stark's troops from New Hampshire were the first to make contact with the enemy. Once Stark had assembled his entire regiment in western Vermont, he reviewed the military situation as it existed at that time and sent out patrols to make contact with the enemy so that he might be able to evaluate their intentions. Burgoyne was at the end of his supply route and had sent out foraging parties of regimental strength to the surrounding territory to confiscate animals, forage and mounts for his German dragoons. One of the largest supply depots in the area was at Bennington. Stark's intelligence indicated that those valuable military stores were the destination of Burgoyne's troops, and Stark took measures to deny the supplies to him. The New Hampshire regiment was quickly marched to Bennington where Stark placed his regiment between the stores and the encroaching British forces in New York.

Drew was attached to the patrol closest to the Bennington storehouse that took them into New York along the shore of the Walloomasac River, a couple of miles from Bennington. They stopped at a mill to grind flour on the river and to check the surrounding area. Suddenly, a full regiment of German dragoons appeared approaching the mill. The two pickets placed in advance of the patrol drew fire from the Germans. They returned fire and quickly retreated towards the mill to warn the patrol. Drew saw no other way than to vacate the mill and report as soon as possible to Stark.

Sporadic skirmishing took place between the two forces until they got out of musket range. Drew had waited behind to account for every man in his patrol. He was quickly being overtaken by one rider who had just fired a shot at him, narrowly missing Drew's head. He then stopped, took careful aim at the German soldier about two hundred feet away with his rifled carbine, and pulled the trigger, knocking the man from his saddle into the dusty roadway. They were able to warn Stark who pulled back from the general area to formulate a plan of action.

That night it rained hard. Stark was busy with his officers sorting out the right tactics to use against the enemy who had occupied a nearby hilltop and was desperately building defenses for the attack that was coming. Their strong position forced Stark to be deliberate and certain of his plan. He was firm in his desire to learn the exact strength and position of the German regiment. To act precipitately could be a major error and very costly to the militia forces.

Stark had about sixteen hundred men under his command from communities in the Berkshires, Vermont, and New Hampshire. Once a plan had been formulated and agreed upon, he was confident that he could defeat the enemy force on the hilltop. His scouting patrols determined that the enemy was about eight hundred men strong. They had several pieces of artillery placed in redoubts on the hill on the north side of the Walloomasac River. It was a logical piece of terrain to defend and would be difficult to overrun. Stark also assumed that they planned to hold in place and wait for reinforcements.

Drew turned his mount into the corral at Stark's main campsite a couple of miles from the Bennington storehouse. Stark called for a council meeting of all officers to review the situation. Both sides had sent out skirmishers to make contact with the enemy and to determine their exact position. Stark developed a plan of attack using maneuver tactics to rout the enemy from their breastworks and trenches on the hillside. He spoke about the large pincer movement he wanted to execute on both sides of the hillside at the same time. One column was to attack the left flank at the same time a second column was to make a wide circular movement to hit the rear and the right flanks of the breastworks as close to the same time as possible. Then, Stark proposed a frontal attack straight up the hill under his command. He would lead the largest number of troops into the battle straight against the redoubts and breastworks. The three pronged attack should cause some confusion within the German command.

They faced well-trained Hessian troops who had a reputation for toughness and determination. They gave as well as they received in any combat situation, and they were seasoned combat veterans. Stark led his column up the hill on horseback. Drew followed at the head of a company from New Hampshire. It was a short vicious battle that lasted less than an hour. All three columns had hit the enemy at the same time – a perfect job of coordination. The speed and three points of contact threw the Germans into disarray, but they fought back tenaciously.

Stark's main line of attack had the mission of knocking out the four small cannons that had been firing into their lines continuously. Drew had made it to the edge of the redoubt for one of the cannons with a squad of militiamen at his side. The difficult climb under fire had drained him of energy and he was sweating profusely. They did not have the advantage of bayonets like the Hessians but that did not lessen their zeal in closing with the enemy. Crouched below the redoubt's wall Drew told the men to be sure their weapons were loaded, primed, and ready to fire.

They then climbed over the wall of the redoubt, firing into the concentration of German artillerymen. They continued, after discharging their weapons, to clear the enemy from the gun emplacement. The surprise of the attackers gave them the advantage. Drew's squad of twelve men did not lose a man. He kneeled beside a wounded German who raised his arms in surrender. Drew quickly reloaded his carbine and removed the musket with attached bayonet from the hands of the wounded German soldier.

A German officer appeared on the edge of the redoubt with a large axe raised to strike a militiaman. Drew raised his carbine and pulled the trigger, watching the man drop the axe and fall within the emplacement. Drew ran to his side to check if he was dead when another German soldier lunged at him with his bayonet, stopping Drew in his tracks. He dropped his precious carbine in the moist soil of the dugout. Drew knew that he was in trouble and was unable to escape the thrust of the sharp bayonet. He cried out, "Oh no!!" as he fell into the mud. The German reached for the carbine as Drew involuntarily pulled a small caliber pistol from his belt and fired into the face of the soldier. He fell on top of Drew. The blood from two enemy combatants flowed freely and mingled together in the mud.

The battle for the hilltop was soon over. The militia forces had obtained a great victory over the determined foe. Drew was pinned beneath the weight of the dead German soldier, and cried out for help. Another wounded soldier next to him echoed his call for help. Several militia men responded to the pitiful cries of the wounded. Soon Drew was taken on a stretcher, with his faithful carbine firm on his hands, to a nearby dressing station.

While he was being attended to, the New Hampshire regiment was caught off guard by a second German regiment attacking from the southwest. It was a close-fought engagement that was decided by the sudden appearance of a Vermont militia regiment that had recently been active in a battle at Hubbardston, Vermont. The two intense actions against Burgoyne's best German troops had deleted the enemy's capability by thirty percent. It was a glorious victory that set the stage for complete defeat of Burgoyne's army at Saratoga a month later. The victory was instrumental in the decision of the French to enter the fight against their long-time foe. The fatal blow to the British came at Jamestown, Virginia. The catalyst that set the wheels of victory in motion was the well-planned operation at Bennington by John Stark.

Drew survived the battle with a large wound slightly below his ribcage. It had been treated quickly enough that it did not become infected. He was confined to a chair or a bed until the wound healed. General Stark was pleased with his performance and visited him at the dressing tent.

"You did well, Drew," said the sad-eyed General. "I'm taking you and several other wounded men back to New Hampshire with me. I need to recruit another regiment for service with the Continental Army so that we can continue the fight under General Gates."

"How soon are you leaving, General?" Drew asked.

"Within a couple of days, son. Your fighting days are over," Stark said, noting the bloody dressings around his midsection. "As a matter of fact, several of the Hessian soldiers have voted to stay in the colonies to live. They're from an area in Hesse County, Germany, very similar to the hilly terrain of New Hampshire and Vermont. I'm prepared to give them a chance to build a new life with us in our new country."

"I'm anxious to go home, General."

"Of course you are, Drew. I, too, dream of that for myself, but first, we've got to be tempered by the fire of a bloody conflict against our brothers to prove ourselves worthy of the honor of determining our own destiny. Rest well, son."

# Chapter Twenty-Three

Drew was most uncomfortable riding in a supply wagon from Bennington to Manchester, New Hampshire, where Stark lived. He bid a hearty good-bye to those few who were going on to Portsmouth. Stark bid Drew and the other wounded men a speedy recovery and the promise of a full life in spite of their grievous wounds. There was a haunting look of regret in his deep-set eyes as he waved a final farewell to them. "Thank you for your courage and sacrifice. I know it's an inadequate token for the suffering you've endured, but it's all I am able to give. You've set a standard of valor that will long be remembered, and you've given it for a cause that is priceless. God Bless my brave soldiers. I am proud to have been your commander."

The slow ride to Portsmouth gave Drew a chance to reflect on the long journey he had traveled ever since he was a small boy on the banks of the Minas Basin. The disruption from his childhood playground had been difficult for him, but it was slight compared to the trauma that must have accompanied his mother and father as they left a part of their hopes and dreams behind only to see their home go up in smoke as they parted the mainland.

The circuitous route that had carried him down the Hudson River was a part of his life that would remain forever locked in his consciousness. All that made the journey tolerable were memories of home as it was now defined on the banks of the Kennebec River. Love of home and all it represented was worth any effort required to defend it from outrageous intrusions of a government out of touch with its people. Once they arrived at Portsmouth, Drew was ecstatic to learn that Captain Jones was tied up to the Market Street wharf waiting to take Drew home. Drew later learned that General Stark had sent a courier by fast horse to the coastal town to have a conveyance of some type available for the wounded soldiers to be taken to their homes.

Captain Jones personally carried Drew to his schooner and placed him in a lounge-like bed secured to the deck at the bow of the ship. "This is for you, Drew. This is one voyage home I want you to remember. Welcome back. Your friends and family have much to be thankful for. We're now leaving Portsmouth for the calm waters of the Kennebec. The last segment of your long journey home is about to begin. Cast off..."

Once the sleek schooner left the confining waters of the Piscataqua River, the familiar landscape along the coast gave Drew a melancholic feeling that watered his eyes. The prominent summit of Mount Agamenticus off the port side was like an old friend welcoming him back. He was thankful that his wounds would not limit his ability to work as he had always done since he was a small boy. At times when he was frightened in the turmoil of combat, his most frequent thoughts always led to home. It was the center of his universe, and he vowed to never leave its comforting environment again.

Memories flowed through his active mind as the sharp bow of the schooner sliced through the blue waters of the Atlantic. Soon the multitude of small islands at the mouth of the Kennebec River welcomed him to familiar surroundings. Captain Jones carefully watched his youthful passenger, observing the traumatic effect that this homecoming was having on his friend. Few know the value of family and home as deeply as a warrior returning to his roots. It takes on a whole new significance that the average person cannot appreciate unless they have also been tested on the field of battle.

Turning into the main channel of the river brought Mudge Jackson's warehouse into view. Not much had changed since Drew passed on his way to war. Soon the familiar boat-building facilities that lined the shores of the river insured that his presence was not a dream but a reality. The schooner gently rubbed against the LeClair dock and was efficiently secured to the mooring posts by the crew. Tears filled his eyes as he viewed the ferry and the tavern from the river.

Captain Jones paused a moment before intruding on Drew's emotional reaction to his homecoming. Two of the crew helped Drew onto the stretcher being held by Captain Jones and another crew member. "Welcome home, Drew."

Drew's mother, father, Ben, and Ana stood anxiously on the porch of the tavern watching him being carried up the stairs of the dock. Through tear-stained eyes, Drew saw Pru running to greet him. She was crying, and tears rolled down her cheeks.

"My dearest friend, Drew, has come home to us. Thank God...," she kneeled to embrace him on the stretcher. "I'm never going to say good-bye to you again. Never... I love you, Drew LeClair, and I have ever since we were young. Your long journey has ended now in my arms..."

THE END

# Other Historical Romance Novels

BY
Clifton LaBree

**A Song for Lisa**   A Historical Romance

This is the story of a young American woman captured by the Japanese in the Philippines, 1941. Like most prisoners, she was brutalized and sadistically treated with a cruel disregard for human life. Three years later, Lisa and her companions had reached the low point of starvation and abuse .....

**Lake of Three Sorrows**   A Historical Romance

A warm spiritually uplifting story of courage, commitment, and sacrifice. This is the story of Dale Cooper, a battle-weary American soldier who served in two world wars.

**Flickering Flame**  (Colonial Series Book One)

A historical novel, about the Cullen family who settled in Portsmouth, New Hampshire, and their participation in events prior to the French and Indian War.  Freedom and opportunity were on the march, but it extracted a heavy price.  Frontier settlers were ruthlessly killed and butchered by rampaging Indians lead by French officers and Jesuit priests who frequently incited them to greater levels of inhumanity...

**Raising the Torch**  (Colonial Series Book Two)

A continuation of the saga from Flickering Flame, Colonial Series book one, of the Cullen family in Colonial Portsmouth. This is a moving story of love and sacrifice when a small colony had the audacity to fight for independence from their motherland...

# Non-Fiction Books

## By

### Clifton LaBree

## New Hampshire's General John Stark, Live Free or Die: Death Is Not the Greatest of Evils

Publisher - Fading Shadows Imprint

A fresh look at one of America's staunchest defenders of liberty and freedom. John Stark was a courageous New Hampshire citizen-soldier who fought in both, the French and Indian War, and the Revolutionary War. His pursuit of leadership excellence on the battlefield distinguished him as one of the most successful combat commanders of the war, and one of the least appreciated.

His selflessness, modest life style, and devotion to the cause of freedom are an inspiration that time has not diminished. He remains today the embodiment of the frugal, independent, and cantankerous New Hampshire Yankee.

## Gentle Warrior, General Oliver Prince Smith, USMC

Published by - Kent State University Press. Kent, Ohio, 2001

The Story of one of the United States Marine Corps best General Officer. His flawless performance in Korea is a story that needed to be told.

# FADING SHADOWS IMPRINT

Fading Shadows Imprint was established to bring to the public books of historical events and portraits of people enduring tragic circumstances of by-gone days. Hopefully, they will generate a deep appreciation and respect for the exceptionalness of the United States of America, and an appreciation for the sacrifice and selflessness of those who valiantly served for liberty and freedom.

The characters are fictional, but the historical events and dates have been seriously researched and are factually presented. Some books feature incidents during the French and Indian Wars as well as the War for Independence.

World Wars I and II are eras rich in stories that beg to be told. I've tried to pay tribute to the collective courage and heroism, often unheralded, that has defined Americans in every engagement. It was a time when the immortality of dreams and aspirations were defended by the blood of young men and women. There is a beautiful monument and cemetery in a small French village where thousands of white crosses and Stars-of-David are set in perfect alignment, honoring thousands of American soldiers who gave their last full measure. A large granite slab bearing mute witness to their sacrifice has the following words chiseled in stone: TIME WILL NOT DIM THE GLORY OF THEIR DEEDS. Another monument reads: VIRTUE AND COURAGE ARE THEIR OWN MONUMENT AND REWARD. Those simple words define the American soldier from the dark days of the Revolutionary War to the present. They are an American treasure, unique in the history of the world.

Every generation has its own signature and characteristics that uniquely define them. The World War II generation is defined by the immortality of the ideals and truth they gallantly defended.

The United States has freely given precious blood and treasure to defend the rights of man to be free, and we have never asked for anything in return. No other nation on the planet has sacrificed so much for the noble virtues of liberty and freedom. We hope that the selections offered by Fading Shadows Imprint will touch your hearts and generate a deeper appreciation and love for our country.